WHEN
TIME
RUNS
OUT

WHEN TIME RUNS OUT

ELINA HIRVONEN

MANILLA

First published in Finland in 2015 by Werner Söderström (WSOY)

First published in Great Britain in 2017 by Manilla Publishing,
80–81 Wimpole St, London, W1G 9RE
www.manillabooks.com

A CIP catalogue record for this book is available from the British Library.

ISBN: 978-1-78658-027-6

2

Also available as ebook

Printed and bound in Great Britain by Clays Ltd, St Ives plc

Manilla Publishing is an imprint of Bonnier Zaffre,
a Bonnier Publishing company
www.bonnierzaffre.co.uk
www.bonnierpublishing.co.uk

PART
ONE

Compassion is an unstable emotion. It needs to be translated into action, or it withers.

SUSAN SONTAG
Regarding the Pain of Others

1

When he was a child, he responded to smiles with a smile. He had two front teeth in his lower jaw and a dimple in his left cheek. When someone smiled at him, his face melted into sunshine and his dimple appeared so soft and delicious that it was tempting to press a finger into it and tickle gently, just to hear the laughter that shook his entire body.

When he sat in his buggy on the tram, strangers would lean over him, smiling and chatting as if they had always known him. He would smile back and point with his chubby fingers at the trees, buses, diggers and street lamps that were visible beyond the windows and say: 'Dat!' And people looked in the direction in which he was pointing, smiled and said: 'What a lovely tree. What a lovely digger. What a lovely motorbike. What a lovely child.'

When the people got off the tram, shielding their faces from the cold wind and the rain, they smiled for such a long time that they no longer remembered why.

2

Helsinki, some time later

He listens again to Pink Floyd's 'Nobody Home' – a song which he has listened to many times each day, for years. When the music ends, everything in him feels light. This is the last time.

His smile is light, his fingers lighter than a fly's wings. He stands in the middle of the city, on a roof which he has always wanted to climb. In his left hand is a semi-automatic small-bore rifle. It was astonishingly easy to steal it from the boot of a car parked beside the shooting range. Ever since he decided to put his plan into action, everything has been astonishingly easy.

This is something I'm good at, he'd thought as he filmed his message and posted it online, packed the rifle into its bag and dressed in a black windcheater, black trousers and soft-soled trainers in which he would be able to climb well. The music moved his body; as he left home he felt like taking a couple of high leaps, leaving the mark of his knuckles in the ceiling with his fist, smashing a hole into the ceiling and marking the wall with the sole of his shoe, running nimbly over the cars, blowing obstacles from his path, like dandelion seeds, feeling so intensely in the moment that nothing could check his speed or his strength.

Now his movements are slower than usual, as if everything were happening underwater. The city is his dream and the sounds of police cars, ambulances and escaping people come distantly, from the other side of the water's surface.

The only thing he can see clearly is the woman he is aiming at. The woman is younger than his mother and so ordinary-looking that she could be anybody. Beside her is another woman, so old that she will probably die soon in any case. He rests the weapon against his shoulder and zooms in on the younger woman's head with the variable scope as if he were making a movie.

The weapon fires when you press the trigger. After the first shot you can fire again without reloading. The trigger is cool beneath his finger. Only a small movement is necessary. The click of the trigger and the kick of the rifle butt against your shoulder. His finger is not trembling. He narrows his eyes. The old woman is shouting something at the younger one, who turns her head away.

They may be mother and daughter, he thinks, as he sets the rifle down for a moment, shaking his arms and taking a deep breath as if after a long dive. Then he raises the rifle again and takes aim at the woman, who is holding her hat as she runs for safety.

3

Laura

I pour some sea salt into an oven dish, scrub a swede clean and set it in the middle of the bed of salt, a round swede-moon. *This will be a good night*, I think. I have studied the art of positive thinking. Eerik, my husband, would laugh if he knew. Everyone who knows me would probably laugh at me. I have always considered that kind of thing stupid, and said so. But now I have decided to fill my mind with positive thoughts, to smile until my brain begins to feel pleasure, and to love myself so much that it will be easy for others to love me too. Otherwise I won't manage. I am fifty-eight years old and completely healthy. I do yoga in the mornings and lift weights in the evenings. I very probably have decades of life left and I have decided to learn to enjoy them.

I am on my way to the university to talk about the climate catastrophe. After that I will fetch Eerik from the airport. In the evening our son Aslak is coming round for dinner.

I lay the table with mismatching plates and put a tall red candle in a wine bottle. It makes me laugh a little: in almost forty years together Eerik and I haven't acquired proper flower vases, candlesticks or complete sets of crockery. Whenever I put a flower or a candle in an empty bottle I remember what it was like when we had little money and plenty of time, what it was like to go to parties thrown by people we didn't know, to wake up to languid Saturday mornings with friends, to order pizza and watch movies whose words we all knew by heart.

I am making Aslak's favourite dish, swede braised until it is soft, then fried until it is sweet and crispy. With the exception of a short period in his youth, Aslak has been a vegetarian all his life, and I am extraordinarily happy about this. As a child he would begin to cry if he saw newspaper advertisements for marinated chicken strips or wafer-thin slices of ham.

'How can anyone live in a world in which living creatures are made into *strips* and *slices*!' he said, his tears falling from his cheeks onto the newspaper. I took the paper from the floor and folded it up, stroked his head and said: 'My love, the world is always changing. You can be part of making it a better place.'

I put the swede in the oven, set the timer for two hours and pull on the clothes that I nearly always wear when

I am lecturing to young people: a simple dress, thick tights and high boots. I glance at the mirror. I have short hair whose iron-grey stripes gleam, depending on the day, bravely or sorrowfully, and there are wrinkles around my eyes – wrinkles I haven't got used to. I hardly use any make-up, but nevertheless, occasionally at the chemist's or in an airport tax-free shop, I find myself reading the label of a new cream and hoping that the cream might be the solution. That it might return me to a time when everything was supposed to be possible.

Soon we are sitting at the sturdy, wooden kitchen table. When Eerik and I moved into this flat, we wanted a long table for a large group of friends. Through the years I often planned dinner parties which we would hold when we had time, when everyday life loosened its grip, when Aslak was going through a better period. I came up with complicated dishes and thought about how to invite friends who didn't know each other. We would eat for a long time and open one bottle of wine after another, the children would say goodnight to everyone in their pyjamas, the evening would continue on into the night and we would talk and laugh and in the morning we would wake up having had too little sleep, but full of energy after a happy evening. Those dinners never happened, and we sat around the big table, a long way from one another.

At that table Aava and Aslak, in their high chairs, ate their first solid food – half a teaspoon of mashed sweet potato. At that table they blew bubbles in their milk glasses and giggled when we told them not to. Years later they sat silently in their places, I talked too much to sustain the conversation, both Eerik and the children chewed their food with glum faces and I was sure that he was thinking of grinding me with his teeth.

I imagine our conversation.

'Aslak. You can't go on like this.'

I say it out loud. The words thud into the room where there is no one but me; they take with them the weight that has spread within me. It has made my breathing laborious and my steps heavy.

'We won't abandon you. We want to help you find somewhere where you can work out what is weighing you down. You're young, sensitive and intelligent and you have a lot to give. We hope that you will have a good life and be able to do the things that are important to you. Don't you want to do that too?'

I think of Eerik's so very familiar posture, which over the years has become ever so slightly stooped, as if he were carrying a burden that was too heavy. Eyes the colour of a winter sky and a gaze that, even in the happiest of moments, has a trace of disquiet. Fine wrinkles at the corners of his mouth, and a chin, covered in grey stubble, which he always rubs when he hears something he doesn't like. I think of Aslak's head, sunk between his shoulders, eyes hidden behind his heavy eyelids, teeth biting his lower lip. I think how everything in him could withdraw still further inside, how his whole body could look for a tortoise's shell to protect it, under which it could hide.

4

A cold wind penetrates my cape-like coat. I wrap it more tightly around my body and try to ring Aslak. I want to make sure that he really is coming, that he is not planning to cancel our arrangement on some pretext whose implausibility would show clearly how little he values me and Eerik.

This happens often. We ask Aslak round, he promises to come, but he does not come. We pretend to be disappointed and suggest a new time, feeling guilty about how relieved we are. Meetings with Aslak are complicated and awkward. I hope for something that will never happen, and Eerik is desperately correct. Even Aslak tries, when he is in the mood, to play the part of a grown-up son. After such occasions Eerik rolls a joint, although he has been trying to give up smoking for almost thirty years. I go for a run, running such a long way in the forest that the world grows dim as if I were drunk.

All the same I go on arranging get-togethers whose spoken aim is to cheer Aslak up and to show that we care. The unspoken aim is that something should finally change.

On Mother's Day I persuaded Aslak to come into the centre of town for brunch. I had booked a table in a restaurant in a renovated banking hall; in front of it seagulls strutted and inside it sat well-dressed families in which even the small children behaved well.

I was wearing a sea-green silk dress, Eerik straight trousers and his best shirt; I had also bought Aslak a new sweater. He arrived with his hair greasy and his skin pale and waxy, dressed in a bobbly T-shirt that smelled of sweat.

'He can't come looking like that,' whispered Eerik, but I hugged Aslak. That day the sky was bright, the smell of the sea was in the air and I had decided to be a happy mother.

I grasped Aslak by the shoulders and piloted him into the restaurant. Eerik paced past me, his eyes on the floor, and the waiter directed us to the table with a smile despite the pungent smell emanating from Aslak.

We ate many tiny starters, a hot main course, cheese and a dessert. Eerik was silent throughout the entire meal and I talked constantly, smiling until my cheeks ached. I passed food to Aslak and ordered drinks, champagne in honour of the occasion, although Eerik raised his eyebrows: in his opinion it was better to drink water with Aslak. I put my arm around Aslak and talked about books and movies he knew nothing about, bands that he had listened to years ago, and memories, the few we had in common that I dared speak about.

'Do you remember when we were on the cycling holiday in Copenhagen? You and Aava sat in a box bike eating melon?

'Do you remember when you learned to skate – you let go of the support and suddenly raced round the rink?

'Do you remember when you programmed your first robot . . . when you wrote an essay and the teacher gave you full marks?'

After the meal I paid the bill, got up with a smile and went to the toilet, locked the door and burst into tears. When I returned, Aslak had already gone. Eerik stood silently by the cloakroom waiting for me, then walked silently out before me.

Aslak doesn't answer. This often happens. When I try to let Aslak take responsibility and don't pay his bills, I cannot reach him for weeks and finally I become so anxious that I take it upon myself to look after all his expenses. I don't tell Eerik about this. He thinks I treat Aslak like a child and that is why he seems stuck in the nest, a fledgling grown enormous who doesn't know how to fly. I leave Aslak a message and run to the metro station.

Beside the entrance is an old beggarwoman on her knees; I turn to give her money and she says thank you in Finnish. I'm startled.

'What a sentimental nationalist you are,' Eerik would say if he was with me. He feels it is perverse of me to avoid gypsy beggars as if I did not see them but to stop whenever I see an elderly Finnish person with a cup in their hand.

When I look more closely at the woman, I notice that she has applied rouge under her sharp cheekbones and wound her scarf around her neck in the manner of French women twenty years ago. For a moment I see myself in her place, in a too-thin coat with a cardboard cup in front of me, trying in spite of the circumstances to look dignified.

I want to speak to my daughter Aava. She lives in Mogadishu and never calls me. Not even when the place where she lives, a small island surrounded by a wall and high watchtowers whose barracks are home to foreign workers, was bombed and her neighbour died.

I am always the one that makes the approach, Aava the one who ends the conversation. Aava leaves and doesn't come back for a long time, pays a quick visit to Finland and only has time for one meeting, even that a brief one, during which she glances around her as if checking for an escape route. When I suggest another meeting, a joint day out or trip, a couple of days when we could get to know each other again, Aava leaves again. She goes to countries where there is too much blood and too little water, to camps quickly jerry-built amid wars, their dry streets swarming with children whose parents were born in the same camp.

I am proud of Aava. My daughter has the courage to go wherever she wants, to survive anywhere. I would like to say this to her. I would also like to say that you don't always have to cope, and when you can't bear it any more, you can come home. I tried once.

'Do you really not get it? It's home I want to stay away from,' Aava said, and I smiled as I learned to do when I was a child and something inside me was crushed.

I love Aava, of course. And admire her. But my admiration is not as pure as I would like it to be. Aava is a better version of myself. She does important work all over the world and lives a life that I thought for years that I would live sometime. Aava doesn't have to negotiate her decisions with anyone, and she doesn't know what it feels like when passion fades. When she comes home, she can close the door and be quiet; she can go whenever she wants to and mourn her own sorrows alone.

5

Ava doesn't respond. The metro station door opens; warmth blows in my face, and the smell of urine that has dried in the corners. *Everything is fine with me*, I think. In my life many things are almost ridiculously fine.

Three young girls are obstructing the escalator and I can't get past them. Hanging from their shoulders are gleaming bags from a designer shop, in their ears headphones decorated with diamonds. Something in their faces makes it clear that it is not worth asking them to step aside. I try to imagine the sounds that are flooding into their ears: are they listening to the streets of Brooklyn or the shores of the Maldives or a secret whispered by a beautiful boy?

The girls' faces glow with health; their bodies are muscular and trim in just the right way. They touch each other gently, and everything about them breathes a deep satisfaction and confidence that the glances directed at them are full of approval.

A year ago a young woman – perhaps the same age as these girls – shot three people in the Helsinki metro. Unlike most other gunmen, she did not leave any clue, any message about her thoughts. According to the policemen who examined the case, there was so little trace of her background that it looked as if she did not exist. She was twenty years old, had dropped out of school, was not in or out of employment, her parents had died, she lived in a flat inherited from her mother, did not socialise or use social media; no one claimed to be her friend. The neighbours said that she went orienteering once a week in the forests near her home. Almost nothing else was known about her.

For a moment pictures of her were everywhere. The pictures showed a slim, long-limbed woman, a face that was good-looking in an ordinary way: high cheekbones and large eyes, a calm gaze and an unsmiling mouth. The pictures stayed in my mind for a long time; I thought about the woman in the darkening forest, a lamp on her forehead, running through the dense spruce forest, along paths fringed with blueberry bushes, full of sounds that no human being had manipulated. I thought of her looking for one cross after another and returning to the red-brick house at the edge of the forest, to the home which, according to the police, looked uninhabited.

The fact that the woman did not leave a message, any explanation for her action, was dumbfounding. In

some extraordinary way we have grown used to killing. We have grown used to the feeling of insecurity
caused by violence, to the grief which everyone wants
to share, to the huddles of candles in the streets and
in the school playgrounds, to the hearts and cloying
ballads of social media which people try to share after
such events. We have learned to deal with death and
a daily insecurity, but not with the silence of a killer.
At a time when everyone is constantly receiving messages, it felt incomprehensibly presumptuous. Not
because she had killed, but because she didn't even
try to explain why.

6

'Hope is an essential part of human nature. If we lose the hope for a better future, what is left to us?'

Before me are fifty environmental science students. They are among the purest and most fortunate of their generation, those to whom the rest of us entrust our hopes. They do not care for alcohol or tobacco, they like cycling, crocheting and hanging out with their friends, dream of time rather than money, hope for a long romantic relationship and switch languages without pause. The same is probably true of their thinking. They have personal carbon monitors and shares in solar energy companies, and they know that if they choose well they can also even make money from protecting the environment.

When I was young, I believed that if we acted together we could ward off environmental catastrophe and bring peace to the world. When I was a little older than these students, deaths on the borders of Europe were still newsworthy events. No longer.

There has been fighting in Egypt, Libya and Syria for so long that no one remembers where it all started, malaria is so widespread in Greece that tourists no longer go there, half of the young people of Spain have moved to Argentina and Chile, and the Swedish prime minister is a former skinhead. In Europe almost half the people have stopped voting in elections. If things go badly for you, you die before you're sixty; if they go well, you can live in a private nursing home until you're 100. We have grown used to snowless winters, endless rain and floods whose power is always surprising. We have grown used to refugees who wander from one European country to another and to the fact that walls are being built round new housing estates.

'Everyone is of equal value!' I shouted as a young demonstrator outside the House of Parliament, believing that, if we only tried hard, if we were to apply ourselves with enough diligence, the world could indeed become a better place for everybody.

When I speak to young people, I am still full of hope. They may succeed where we did not. What looks now like an inevitable move towards the destruction of humanity may develop in unexpected directions. We may create versions of the future, imagine alternative worlds, new visions; one of them may one day come true. But we cannot be certain. The power of humankind may surprise us not only in destructiveness and selfishness, but also in wisdom, reason and the creation of the new.

'Nothing is more pointless than to imagine the entire world revolving around you,' said my grandmother when we were travelling by tram to the centre of town. She always got up to offer a seat to people who were younger than her but who looked more tired.

'Your generation has everything most people in the world will never have. That is why you do not have the right to think only of yourselves.' Granny grew up in a little farmhouse with eleven siblings and was present, as a child, when two of them were buried. As a young woman she worked in a factory, and later as maid to a rich man; she was the first to wake and the last to go to bed in the house, but there was one thing she would never compromise over.

'If you want to achieve something in life, you have to be content when you look in the mirror,' she said. She stood in front of the little mirror in the hall, adjusting a gossamer-fine net over her hair and carefully brushing mascara onto her eyelashes, which curved so beautifully that in another place and time her face might have made her famous. In the tram, Granny held on to the pole with a hand clad in a pale-brown nappa leather glove; from her wrist rose the spicy scent of perfume. I stood next to her, trying to stay upright in the swaying carriage.

My granmother could have been something completely different, I thought. The idea was dazzling. She could have written books or acted in films. She could have defended oppressed people or participated in decisions about the country's affairs. Instead, for most of her life, she prepared food for a man whose sense of taste was so impaired that he could not distinguish between fish and meat, polished silver spoons and ironed shirts which had to be washed once a week and which always had to be hung up neatly. All the same, Granny always behaved as if she had been able to do whatever she wanted. If life was a disappointment to her, she hid this from everyone else.

At the university, I talk about a subject that I have been talking about for all my adult life. About why climate change is treated as if it were merely a question of practical economics, although the bigger questions are about ethics.

'Your generation will solve the great ethical questions of humanity,' I said at the beginning of my lecture, and the students raised their gaze from their reading devices and concentrated on me, fifty pairs of eyes whose brightness lit up the entire space.

'Do we consider the lives of people who live far away as being as important as our own? Do we care what kind of conditions future generations will live in? Do we have the right to seek the short-term advantage of a minority regardless of what it means for the majority of the human race now and in future decades?'

I show the students pictures of Arctic areas where bright water glitters beneath the ice sheet, or the Amazon, where dry land is conquering the rainforests, or the Mali village covered by desert sand which women leave, carrying their children.

The students look at the images in silence, their fingers stroking the edge of their desks. Their serious faces still have a hint of the roundness of childhood.

'Many people have decided that there is no longer any hope,' I say.

'But sustaining hope when problems seem impossible is the most important thing there is.'

The last picture is of Canada. It shows hands in blue plastic gloves, covered in oil. Environmental activists from all over the world are cleaning up an oil spill in the Arctic with native people and workers from the oil company. I look out of the window at the street lamps, which are coming on, pull my mouth into a zip-tight smile and seek the words that I wish to believe myself.

'Do you remember that catastrophe?' A few of the students nod.

'For me it was a kind of turning point,' I continue.

'Before it happened, I talked and wrote continually about how destructive it would be to drill in the Arctic.

I met ministers, members of parliament and CEOs of oil companies. Each one of them promised to familiarise themselves with the studies I presented them with. They smiled at me as if I were a child. When this happened, I was enraged. I thought the human race had no future. I wanted to go and live alone on a faraway island. But when I saw pictures of people who had arrived from different parts of the world starting to cleanse the area together, I realised that giving up hope was a symptom of my own inability to imagine a better world, not on what could really happen.'

As I put on my coat I glance at my phone. Eerik is at Heathrow.

See you soon. I've missed you. ♥ My Eerik has at last, at the age of fifty-nine, learned how to use the heart emoji.

We met at an old gravel pit almost forty years ago. Eerik had a camera round his neck and was explaining how the derelict area could be transformed into a meadow, the gravel pits made into ponds where local residents would be able to swim. Eerik was wearing a frayed jumper and gumboots; he had shaved his head but left a few long hairs at the back of his head. I was reading environmental politics and was funding my studies by writing articles for political papers. Eerik was studying to be an architect and his diploma project was the renovation of the gravel pit into a park for local residents. We arranged an interview at the spot where Eerik was taking photographs for his project.

When Eerik loped up in his dirty boots to shake me by the hand, his eyes glowing with his imagined landscapes, I did not want to let go of his hand. We walked round the vast wasteland and Eerik told me about a Swedish mine which had been transformed into a fabulously lit open-air theatre, and an English landfill site that had been planted with grass. From above, the lawn looked like a woman's body.

'I am really inspired by the idea that a run-down, even devastated, landscape can be reshaped to become beautiful,' Eerik explained, drawing curves in the air with his hand as if he were painting the landscape he was designing. Our arms touched; Eerik smelled of the forest and of sweat, and I grasped his face with both hands.

We undressed each other at the bottom of the gravel pit; the sharp stones scratched our backs. We took the train back to my home and made love many times; on the other side of the window we could hear the chirping of wagtails, the sounds of drunks and police sirens. We spent three days and three nights together; my flat smelled of wine, sweat and lavender oil, and the sun shone all the time.

I never liked dating. After I moved away from home, I wanted clear boundaries between myself and other people. I wanted to keep my mind and my body as a sealed package; I was prepared to concern myself with the future of the globe, but not with the private sorrows of any one person. I took men home with me, friends and strangers, but at the point when they began to talk about dating I stopped returning their calls.

With Eerik, we never talked about dating. He arrived in my life like an early spring, and suddenly the world was full of light. When we weren't together, I thought about his skin. I cycled to lectures thinking about my hand running up and down his belly and nearly ran a dog over. When we were together, I undressed him. We ate quickly, we went for quick runs and sometimes to the cinema, but all the time I was waiting for the moment when I could grab the hem of his shirt. I didn't want to meet his friends or introduce him to mine. I wanted to keep him in a warm room with David Bowie playing and spend the whole day naked.

During our years together I have often hated Eerik. I have wanted to go away and never return. I have gone away, and I have always returned. I have been in love with another person, and I know that Eerik has too, even though he has never told me.

But nevertheless, after all the moments of uncertainty and weariness, after all the nights filled with lonely wandering, after all the disappointed glances and concealed bitterness, I always cheer up when I see Eerik's face in the crowd. At the end of a long day I wait for the time when we can cook together, open a bottle of wine and talk about the details of the day that have made us laugh and the sorrows we conceal from others, and ask questions to which only the other knows where to look for answers.

As I tie my scarf I imagine Eerik walking to the arrivals hall of the airport pulling behind him the suitcase on which I have written his name. Eerik knows me better than anyone else, and sometimes I have to leave for precisely that reason. We embrace in the hall amid the other people, I press my face against his ancient sweater, inhaling the scent of coffee and aeroplane; my clothes carry the scent of the autumn weather and he brushes away a leaf caught on my coat collar. We decide to take the bus to the centre of town and walk home from there, to stop for a drink or just walk hand in hand; in the biting cold weather he's the warmth of a familiar hand, and a shared sense of humour cultivated over many years, brings us home long before we have opened the door.

Eerik has spent a week in Zambia, where he is planning the transformation of an old copper-mining area into a public park.

'Children could plant their own trees here,' he explained, his drawings before him, his eyes gleaming in a way that makes everything around him shine. I want to hear everything about the trip. I want to see if he has remembered to protect his face with sun cream or whether his nose is peeling again.

In the university corridor a teaching assistant approaches me. I wave to her and she grabs my hand hard, as if one of us were in danger of falling.

'They're asking for you,' she says, nodding at two policemen standing by the wall.

7

Aava

'I do not have the strength for grief. Doctor, please let me die too!'

The woman may be younger than me, but her face, framed by its violet scarf, is crisscrossed with wrinkles. The fingers that squeeze my wrist are bony and hard.

'I am so sorry.'

I have said this many times. The words have no meaning. I have nothing else to give.

The woman's daughter had eyes the colour of toasted almonds and an intense gaze. When I visited the village for the first time, the girl broke away from the giggling crowd of children that had followed me at a safe distance and approached me as if I were an animal that might attack or run away.

The village children formed themselves into a straggling line from which each of them stepped forward in turn to be weighed and let me measure the thickness of their arms. I noticed the girl who was walking beside the queue, although she turned away as soon as I glanced at her.

'What is your name?' I asked. For the village children, I had practised a soft, calm way of speaking so that the presence of a white adult would not frighten them.

'Haweeyo.'

'A lovely name. Would you like to come and help?'

The eyes of the other children in the queue turned from me to the girl. She stood still for a moment, then adjusted her scarf and came to me, picked up the tape and listened intently while I explained which part of the arm should be measured.

'Auntie. I would like to be a doctor like you.' The whisper was so soft that at first I did not hear it at all.

It was the first calm moment of the day. The last child had left. I was packing my things and going through the children's health cards with the nurse. The girl stood next to the wall of the hut, drawing circles in the earth with her toes.

'What, my love?'

'I want to be the same as you. I want to fly in an airplane and give children peanut butter,' the girl said clearly, and the nurse, too, looked at her, smiling.

'You could work with me,' the nurse said cheerfully.

'We three could make miracles happen!' said the girl solemnly. The light of the setting sun filtered through the thatched roof; from outside came the song of the sacred ibis. We three. How beautiful the thought was.

The village elders approach the woman. The men wear long white garments, cool in the heat, henna-dyed beards and penetrating gazes beneath their furrowed brows. I follow them to the village chief's house, sit on a carpet on the floor and gratefully accept a warm Sprite. Beneath my scarf, my bulletproof vest and my long-sleeved shirt, drops run along my skin: insect slime. A nauseating taste rises in my throat. I swallow it as I have learned to swallow in markets stinking of fish that has been left in the sun. I taste the sugary drink and prepare to answer all their questions.

'The doctor was away too long.'

'I am sorry,' I say again. My throat is dry. I have to cough. I raise my hand in front of my mouth and try to do so quietly, but the sound is loud, my body shakes, tears come to my eyes.

'It is not enough. You fly here when it suits you, arrive full of self-importance and give instructions. But when something bad happens we are always left alone.

'If you had come earlier, she might have survived.'

'I wanted to come,' I say. My voice is clear and steady again. 'But after the murder, the security department would not let anyone come here.'

'But no foreigners were killed.'

'The local doctor died. The murder was completely absurd.'

'A quarrel about a land deal.'

I squeeze my hands, hidden by my long sleeves, into fists. The murdered doctor had clear eyes and a firm handshake. He told children who were frightened of injections a joke about a man who had grown up in the village and went to the United States to meet some relatives. At the airport the man's mother said, 'May Allah open doors for you.' When the automatic doors at the new country's airport opened for the first time, the man smiled happily. Allah was with him.

'His name was Suldaan. He was my colleague.'

'And once more a child died, a child who otherwise would have stayed alive,' said the village chief. The veins in his neck were as thick as a lizard's tail, his fingers as twisted as the staff with which he tapped the ground as he spoke.

'I would like to do much more,' I say. 'But as long as the security situation is as it is, there are very few opportunities.'

When I rise to leave, the village chief grasps my hand. I am startled. In this village men never shake hands with women. I squeeze the man's hand. His palm is soft, even though everything else about him is furrowed and hard. The aeroplane awaits me on the narrow runway in the midst of the dense scrub. The khaki nose of the plane glimmers through the dark green leaves. Under the patchy paint, rust is visible. I do not wish to think about the condition of the parts of the plane I cannot see. The children run after me in a squealing crowd, spreading their arms into wings and shouting:

'Sister, take us with you!'

The village chief takes a stick from the ground and uses it to drive the children away, gently but firmly.

8

I close my eyes. Gerard presses his thumbs into my shoulders, into the spots where hard knots lurk. The pain pierces down to my toes. I press my teeth together and let the tears rise to my eyes.

'Am I pressing too hard?' Gerard asks.

'Harder.'

My shoes lie where I left them, at the door of the hut; their soles are caked with dry mud, the laces red with sand. My long skirt, my scarf, my bulletproof vest and my helmet are bundled up on the bed. I took them off as soon as I came inside and stood in the middle of the room in my most modest bra and knickers, my skin pale, even though the sun shines here constantly at this time of year, under my arms the pressure marks left by the bulletproof vest. I always use the same underwear on field trips. The reason is al-Shabaab. They may appear as I am working, point their guns at the villagers and kidnap me. If they take a woman prisoner, she is likely to be raped. Kidnappings do not take place very often at the moment, but being kidnapped is possible on every field trip. That is why I always think about it before I leave. And I always think about it when I return to work from holiday. Every time I wonder whether I am ready to take the risk. Is my job worth it? Up until now I have concluded that it is. But if one day I end up in the hands of al-Shabaab's soldiers, I want my underwear to be modest, and as ugly as possible.

When I returned from the village, I phoned Gerard straight away.

'Can you come? I don't want to be alone.'

As always, Gerard came, smiling as warmly and innocently as a child, in a way which I find at the same time charming and irritating, made some tea and offered to massage my back.

Dark hairs grow on the backs of Gerard's hands. He has black, curly hair and a face that is handsome in a male-model way. When we make love, he asks, 'What would you like?' so tenderly and annoyingly that sometimes I would just like to slip away and read a book.

When flirting, Gerard hints at unusual pleasures, but he touches me as conventionally as if he were sitting an exam. When I lie naked next to him, I often wish I were different from the way I am. I wish I were a softer and more open woman, one who could love Gerard as unconditionally as he deserves to be loved. Sometimes, at such moments, I hear Gerard's mother's footsteps on the other side of the wall, as clearly as if they were real.

Gerard is the only child of a French diplomatic family. He was a curly-haired, cherubic boy who spent his childhood in various African countries, spoke three languages before he learned to read, ate with a knife and fork while he was still in his high chair, on safari trips he sat in a miniature canvas chair wearing sunglasses during meals, looking longingly at the fuzzy-headed children who were kicking a football made of old T-shirts.

'Darling, don't drip mayonnaise on the chair,' Gerard's mother would say, cleaning up the drop of mayonnaise that had fallen from a piece of bread before it could leave a stain, spreading more sun cream onto her son's forehead and promising that they would buy ice cream on the way home.

Gerard hated his canvas chair and did not want any ice cream. He wanted to be with the children whom he saw playing, laughing, running and squabbling around him, whether in South Africa, the Congo or Senegal. He looked on as the other children flitted around in flocks, wrestled, hugged and giggled, on the other side of the fence or the car window, and was too gentle to do anything but nod at his mother, who grasped him by the shoulders and took him inside to watch a movie.

I love that curly-headed boy watching other children from the outside. For the sake of that boy I wish that I could love the grown-up Gerard more.

Gerard's fingers become softer, slipping downwards from my shoulders, caressing my back and my sides.

'Massage me some more,' I say. I sound irritable, although I try to hide it.

'Am I doing something wrong?'

Gerard is never angry with me. That often makes me want to say something that will definitely hurt him, will make him lose his temper and shout out loud for once. Now Gerard's voice has its familiar, annoying tone. *He blames me, even though he doesn't say so*, I think. I say nothing.

When I was a child, father and mother would argue endlessly about the way they looked at each other, the words they used and each other's tone of voice.

'What do you mean?'

'Why?'

'Why are you looking at me like that?'

'What do you mean?'

'Accusingly.'

'I didn't.'

'Yes, you did.'

The arguments usually happened at night and they would often go on until the pale light of morning came through the gap between the curtains. My parents thought that Aslak and I were asleep, but we were always woken by the arguments. When we were little and still slept in the same room, Aslak came into my bed and I made a nest for us with the blankets, stroked my little brother's petal-soft hair and read *Finn Family Moomintroll* out loud.

I was certain that if Gerard and I were still together in ten years' time, we would argue in the same way. Sometimes I picture us older, surveying each other like dogs forced to fight, always ready to attack. Those images turn my stomach, like water drawn from a dirty well. They are one of the many reasons I do not want to sustain a relationship with Gerard or any-one else. I yearn for another person's skin and the demands of his touch, not a life partner. The mere thought of couples' dinners, date nights or working at a relationship makes me feel ill. I want to work for starving children, not at a relationship languishing for lack of passion.

'No. My shoulders feel ... Everything feels so pointless.'

'What do you mean?'

'While I was away, a child died in the village.'

'What of?'

'Diarrhoea.'

'It wasn't your fault.'

'Her name was Haweeyo. It means the elevated one.'

'In these conditions what we can do—'

'She was perhaps eight or nine years old. She wanted to be a doctor.'

'You need to think about all the children who don't die.'

I squeeze Gerard's hand so tightly that it must hurt him.

'Sometimes I think it would be better if they died too.'

'Don't talk like that,' Gerard says. A red flush spreads across his neck. Polite, well brought-up Gerard can talk endlessly about literature, politics and the influence of *terroir* on the taste of wine, but blushes every time someone violates the limits of a respectable conversation with wrong opinions or words that are intended to wound.

'What joy does what we do bring anyone?' I ask quietly. 'What joy is there in the medicines and peanut paste that will help them survive one famine, only to wait for the next, lurking immediately on the other side of the dry season, unless al-Shabaab kidnaps them to be sex slaves or soldiers before that happens?'

'You mustn't think like that.'

'Why not?'

'You can't set a value on anyone's life according to what happens in it.'

'But that's what we're supposed to think!' My voice rises to its highest pitch. A hysterical woman. 'That's what we're paid for, so that we can buy an apartment in Paris or Helsinki and rent it out while we're here. We know that we can pack it in whenever we want to and that we won't have to worry about anything. After a couple of years' work we get a pension on which we can live for the rest of our lives.'

'This job is not about the money.'

'It's a pretty good perk.'

Gerard's thumb presses so strongly into the hard part of my muscle that the pain flares through my entire body.

'But for you that's not what it's about. Or for any of us,' says Gerard. 'Isn't that the important thing?'

'What's it about, for me? Or us?'

'Helping.'

'Helping? Who on earth are we? Children from the last millennium? Hey, let's go and help suffering Africans!'

'Don't be mean.'

'I know you mean well. You always mean well. But you know as well as I do that we can't help anyone here. And the word itself, helping, what does it mean? We're not even pretending to help, are we, but improving conditions together with the local people.'

'And when we don't succeed in changing the whole world, it's pointless to be happy about the fact that we can sometimes save a few children from death?'

'And then kill them just by making a mistake.'

'I'm sorry. I didn't mean that.'

'Are we disagreeing? Everyone here is going on about how nothing will change. But we stay here, each for our own reasons. I believe that all those reasons are selfish ones, however much we try to pretend otherwise.'

'You're not really that cynical.'

Gerard strokes my hand. He sounds so unhappy that for a moment I consider giving up just for his sake, leaving the lonely, curly-haired cherub in peace. But I can't give up. These things have been gnawing away at me for a long time, but speaking them aloud is never appropriate. Workers who come from abroad do not wish to hear this kind of thing; during work time they talk about work and during time off about things that take one's thoughts as far as possible from here. The local people do their work in much more difficult conditions than we do, often at the risk of their safety or of their lives. They must believe in what they are doing, and it would be ridiculous for someone like me to complain to them about frustration. Now my words felt cleansing, like coming out of a fever at the end of a long bout of flu.

'This isn't cynical. It's cynical to argue that we're doing something important. That we're doing something indispensable, when in reality we get paid incredibly well for artificially keeping people alive, people who have no future.'

'You can't define what the future means for an individual. Cultures are so different. People can be happy, even—'

'... If they have nothing? Come on. That's the world's oldest and laziest way of salving a bad conscience. Ooh, lovely, poor and happy savages!'

'Material goods aren't the only way of defining the meaning of life.'

'Don't. You're too clever for that. Any one of us would kill themselves rather than change places with anyone here.'

I'm shouting. Tears are welling up in my eyes.

'But we're here to make something happen. In the next generation things may be better.'

'Do you really think so? How long have we been here? Ten years? Twenty? Thirty? What has happened in that time?'

'What's the alternative?'

Gerard's voice is a whisper. He stops massaging me and sits on the bed beside me. His neck is sweaty with emotion. He has broad shoulders, big hands and nails which he always keeps short. I hug him tight. I press my face into his coarse, curly hair, which smells of soap imported from France.

'Yes,' I say into his hair. 'We can't even contemplate the alternative. We can't imagine a world in which these people or their children could have any hope.'

'This country is full of people who spend all their time trying to achieve something good. We are here so that they are not left alone. If we left, it would be much harder for them to work. You know that as well as I do.'

Gerard ends the conversation by kissing me, softly and tentatively as always. I undo my ugliest bra myself.

9

The restaurant's lights are too bright. I almost never wear make-up here, but now I wish I had applied some powder. Under the bright lights my face feels too bare for the gazes of others.

The restaurant is not a restaurant but the dining hut of our barracks. In the middle is a row of long tables with benches on either side; the food is camel meat, rice and lukewarm tea. The same food as at almost every meal. Outside the walls many people have nothing.

At the door Gerard lets go of my hand. Public displays of affection are not approved of here. We have been in this country for long enough for the rules to be easy to remember. You can only walk in the area within the walls; if you leave it, you must wear a bulletproof vest and helmet. Women and men dress soberly and modestly, alcohol is expensive and it is drunk in secret. On holiday in Europe I walk the streets from morning till night, dress in sleeveless shirts and drink beer on park benches. I do things that I used to do before

I came here, but they no longer feel the same. Everything that was once ordinary has taken on unfamiliar tones. When I do something that was once everyday and happened unnoticed, I see myself at the same time from the outside, as if someone from this country were watching me. She sits in a beauty parlour stretching out her legs for a slender-wristed woman to massage them. She runs through a dark town listening to the guitar music of the Touaregs and does not notice that the seams of her trousers are about to split. She takes home a man whom she met for the first time two hours ago. She orders in expensive food and reads a book in bed, even though it is only lunchtime.

The cook ladles rice and sauce onto the tin plates. I have been here for so long that, without my asking, she gives me exactly the amount I like – a little rice and a lot of sauce.

'*Mahadsanid*,' I say, trying to smile. I have learned enough Somali to be able to play with the village children and to have simple conversations with the adults. Many of the foreigners here do not know the language at all; that is why the cook and the guards smile at me for a little longer than they do at the others.

I slide onto the bench beside Gerard. Already there are two workers from an Italian refugee organisation and the director of a British food-aid charity who is always looking for a job elsewhere. The bench is too short; the smell of food and the touching thighs and

the scents of sweat, hair gel, shaving cream and mois-
turiser make my stomach churn, like earth so softened
by floods that the trees fall to the ground.

Haweeyo loved football, could run faster than anyone
else in the village and wanted to make sure none of the
village children died when she grew up. Her posture
was so upright that it looked as if she were balancing
an invisible burden on her head, something wide and
heavy which must not be broken. Her eyes were intelligent and her movements focused, and her laughter
sounded like the tinkling of wind chimes on a calm
evening when someone runs past. She did not want to
get married.

'I don't want to stop growing,' she said as she helped
me sort through the children's health cards. 'Everyone
thinks that after the wedding the woman is supposed
to shrink and leave space for the man to grow,' she
explained, passing me the cards, which she had stacked
in a neat pile.

'You only have one life. I want to decide what I do
myself.'

Her neck was as long and slim as a heron's; the muscles of her arms were strongly curved. Even though
she was still a child, she looked for a moment as if everything in her were sculpted from strong timber swept
by storm winds.

Her death was my fault. I could have saved her. I knew that there had been heavy rain in the village and that diseases had spread. I should have returned earlier, should have defied the security department's ban. I had always managed here, and I would have managed now. I should at least have left the village nurses more nutritional supplements. I should have assessed the situation more quickly, done something differently.

When I left the village for the last time before Haweeyo's death, she walked beside me to the plane, raising her hand to shield her eyes and staying to watch as the plane rolled down the runway, which had been cleared amid the brush, even when the other children had run off to go on playing or working. She dreamed of many things but got nothing. Everyone says that it was not my fault, but I know it was.

'You're still thinking about her,' says Gerard.

'Yes.'

'Why her, in particular?'

I don't know what to say. In this country you see people die all the time. Many of my local colleagues have died in car-bomb attacks; everyone has lost a member of their family. Children I have cared for are constantly dying of malnutrition, al-Shabaab attacks or illnesses that are curable elsewhere. Those who survive continue their lives shrunk by fear and violence; often their brains have been irreversibly changed by hunger.

In the first weeks, I wept every night. After work each day I curled up in bed, thrusting a fist into my mouth because the walls of my quarters do not insulate sound and crying until all my limbs hurt. Then I realised how ridiculous I was. No one in this country benefits from my tears. I have come here to work, and if I do my best I can even be of a little use. I stopped crying, imagining a tough bubble between myself and the world, and concentrated on my work. At night, though, I still had nightmares in which children's faces floated towards me, unsmiling mouths and eyes which would not look away.

I admire my colleagues here. They mourn each death together but still go to work in the morning, run through the day's tasks and set to. They say they are doing what they can and that they laugh whenever possible. Here people put their own lives in danger to save a neighbour's child and go on with their lives after attacks and bombings, teaching their children how to read at home and returning to the market to sell fruit and fish. They walk with their heads held high, following what is happening around them, discussing politics and life, their eyes bright, pausing to admire the town when it is gilded by sunset and laughing many times a day. I admire their ability to function, their power to sustain hope, their courage to maintain their dignity, both their own and that of others.

I, too, try to concentrate on action. I try to do everything as well as I can, because the only meaning is in what I can achieve. My tears and my nightmares do not help anyone. My pain is the angst of the privileged. The small minority that has grown accustomed to thinking that dreams can be realised, and if that doesn't work, you can demand better. A minority that can say, 'Everything depends on yourself' and 'Good things happen to good people' without a hint of irony and which loses its capacity to function when it finds itself in a situation in which bad things continually happen and almost nothing depends on yourself.

Now, suddenly, on account of a girl with a neck like a heron's, everything collapses. I need to get away. I don't know where. On holiday in Europe, images of this country slip without warning into my mind. I see in the human crowds of Paris, Rome, London or Copenhagen the faces of dead children; I listen to my friends' conversations about music or books and start to cry without being able to explain why. All the same, I would like to be able to pack my bags and travel without a destination, going through unknown countries, concentrating only on how to reach the next place and where to sleep the next night, on border checks and darkening roads strictly controlled by police patrols.

'Aava! Did you hear what's happening in Helsinki?'

Eva, a worker for a Swedish refugee organisation, joins me and Gerard with her tray. In the brightly lit, non-air conditioned canteen she looks as effortlessly beautiful as Swedes always do, as if she had arrived here simply to see what it was like.

'What's happening?' asks Gerard. My tongue swells in my mouth. Suddenly all my words are Finnish words, and no one here understands Finnish.

'Someone is shooting people in the centre of Helsinki.'

'What?'

'There were shootings in other places at the same time, London and Paris at least. They've posted messages on the internet about the culling of humanity.'

'The what?'

'The culling of humanity. That there are too many of us, we're using up too many natural resources, that kind of thing.'

'No.' The whimper of an animal with a broken leg. My voice. Gerard squeezes my hand hard.

'Sick.' Good-natured, shocked Gerard. He speaks four languages fluently, but the grammar of hate is unfamiliar to him.

'It's as sick as could be,' says Eva. 'They use real issues to justify this . . . slaughter.'

'Where's the news story?' asks Gerard, leaning over Eva to look at her phone. Their heads are close together, their hands tanned and beautiful.

I get up. I stagger, jolting the table, and tea spills onto Gerard and Eva's feet.

'*Anteeksi*,' I say in Finnish, using the hem of my skirt to mop up the lukewarm drink. Gerard takes my hand. I tear myself away so violently that I bang my back on the table opposite.

'Darling. Are you OK?'

'I need to talk to my mother.' I say it in French, so Eva won't understand.

'Shall I come with you?'

Gerard gets up to follow me. I shake my head, walking past the long table and the people who are looking at me in confusion. My arms and legs are awkward and heavy. I remember the hippo that found its way onto a restaurant terrace in a Tanzanian nature reserve where Gerard and I were on holiday. Its feet made holes in the floor and every time it turned round it broke something. Time at the restaurant tables stood still; the restaurant guests paused, forks in mid-air, to stare at the creature, which was sweet when seen in the river from a distance but threatening in a small space. The children of the neighbouring village had been sailing toy boats at the point where the hippos accessed the water. One of them had been trampled by the herd of hippos. The waiters ushered the hippo out quietly as if they had whispered to it. Now I understand how terrified the creature must have been.

I open the door, step outside and see the guard walking round the garden, rifle in hand, the velvety black sky and the stars, which always shine more brightly here than at home.

10

My mother doesn't answer. For a moment I imagine her at work, talking to an eager audience about things that I hated when I was a child; they always seemed more important than me. I imagine my mother's greying hair and the clothes that she wore from one decade to the next. For a moment I am a child again, angry because she never saw me properly. *I will never be like that*, I thought, looking at her behind the computer, lost in her work, always ungroomed-looking, concentrating on saving the world, incapable of being happy. My wardrobe, even here, is full of white, well-cut shirts; I iron their collars before going to work. My mother does not even own an iron.

My fingers are cold, even though the wind that blows from the garden is warm. I wrap a fine scarf around my shoulders, pulling the ends so tightly that breathing is difficult; I tie it in a knot and walk towards the far wall, where I can hear the sea. I take a wrong step on the dark path and my leg slips painfully. I rub my ankle and go on.

The smell of burnt wood wafts through the air. From the bar on the other side of the garden comes talk in English and French. Gerard and Eva probably went there from the canteen. I imagine them drinking ginger beer, side by side on the narrow bench, their voices lowering as they talk about what is happening in Helsinki now.

'What's wrong with Aava?' Eva will ask, and Gerard will shrug his shoulders.

'Sometimes she's just very . . . individual.'

At the end of the garden is the gardener's family's tiny house, in its garden a pink Hello Kitty scooter which a Japanese doctor brought the children. I go past the house to the wall, crouching at the roots of the hibiscus bushes at a spot where the children have built a den. Beside my feet are a doll's blanket and some little porcelain coffee cups.

We were in the playroom, just the two of us. Aslak was wearing yellow-and-black-striped pyjamas that had shrunk in the wash; he looked like a little tiger cub. He asked me to help him make desert fox ears for his head, and paint dark fox eyes on his face, with sharp teeth at the corners of his mouth. Against my fingers, Aslak's skin was as soft as whipped cream. I painted the animal features on top of his own. Something about it horrified me. Aslak was my laughing little brother who, after showering, stuck his tummy out against my tummy and wanted to play fat men. When he asked me to draw a fox's features on his face, it felt as if my drawing exposed something that was hidden inside him.

'Why can't you be a prince?' I asked.

'I'm a desert fox princess,' Aslak replied, and his gaze belonged both to him and to someone else. 'I save anyone who is in distress.'

I nodded in annoyance, putting on a dress with a gold hem and setting a silver tiara with pink-and-turquoise stones on my head.

I spread Granny's old lace scarf on the little table and set on it porcelain cups and a wooden cake with pieces, attached with stickers, that you could cut with a little knife. Aslak grabbed a flashing light sabre and invited Mum and Dad to the cake party. For once they came, hand in hand and laughing, putting on crowns and cloaks and saying they were the kings of the neighbouring land. Sitting on the floor, they drank coffee from the porcelain cups.

Aslak soon got tired of the game and began to run round the room, howling like a desert fox. I ran too and Dad and Mum chased us, grabbing us with a hug and tickling us under the arms and on the tummy, and Aslak and I laughed bubbles of laughter which tinkled in the room even after we had gone to sleep.

From: Aslak

To: Aava

I know you're not really interested, but there isn't anyone else I can tell. I'm part of something. Can you look after Mum and Dad? I don't want any of you to come to any harm. This is my own private thing.

That was a message I received from Aslak two weeks ago. I replied straight away.

From: Aava

To: Aslak

What are you talking about? Of course I'm interested! Call me!

From: Aava

To: Aslak

Hi. Could you send me a message? I'm really worried.

From: Aava

To: Aslak

Hi. I really hope you're not doing anything stupid. I love you.

From: Aava

To: Aslak

We need to talk. I can get some leave and come to you.

ANSWER ME!!!

I thought about the message all the time. I thought about it at work and in the evening with Gerard, talking in the neatly swept clay hut with the local nurses and measuring the arms of the quietly waiting children in the sun with the faded tape measure that I brought here from home.

I wanted to tell someone. I wanted to shift the burden away from myself, to tell someone who would know what to do. But what would I have said? And to whom? Aslak has sent the same kind of message before, many times. *I'm going to kill myself. I'm going to kill you. I'm going to kill anyone at all.*

At first I kept the messages. I rang the police and the psychiatric hospital, the therapist whom Aslak used to see a long time ago. I explained the situation and asked what I should do.

'Nothing,' they said.

'If there isn't anything else.'

'If he doesn't want help himself.'

'There's nothing we can do in this situation.'

In the end Aslak always answered. He behaved as if he hadn't ever sent the message, as if everything was completely normal. He wanted to talk about music or politics, which he always followed. And everything from before turned into a dream, into my own imagining, which was real only to me.

Every time it happened, I decided to let go. I decided to disengage from Aslak, whose distorted reality also distorted my reality, in whose presence I always became once more a little child, fearful for her little brother.

I woke before sunrise and ran around the garden by the walls for so long that the sky was pale and the air too hot to get out of breath. I worked, watched movies, did press-ups and abdominal muscle exercises in the evenings and tried to love Gerard more than I did. I thought about Aslak. I didn't think about him. Dad or Mum asked if I could contact him and I said I was busy, although I wanted to say fuck you. And in the end at some stage one of us contacted the other and it all began again.

I was certain Aslak would reply this time too. At some point he would reply again.

Days and weeks went by. Aslak did not reply.

I press my face against the cool wall. Behind it I can hear the sea's comforting roar. Just a little way away from here sail the heavily armed boats of former fishermen, young men who once threw stones on the shore and are now accustomed to kidnapping, torturing and killing other people.

PART TWO

The woman said: now I'm going to tell you a grown-up story.
I'm going to tell it because I'm a child, and in pain.
I am going to tell it for me and for you.

SAILA SUSILUOTO
Siivekkäät ja Hännäkkäät
('The Winged and the Tailed')

11

Much earlier

Laura

'Could we?'

'No.'

'Why?'

'Because.'

'It would be lovely.'

'I don't want to.'

'Why not?'

I began to cry. Vexation strained Eerik's face. I cried quite a lot in those days; Eerik never.

'Your crying is the soundtrack of our relationship,' Eerik said when he got cross with me. 'As if it were a party and someone was putting on the same piece over and over again, and no one wanted to hear it.'

Eerik drew away, pulled the sheet over himself and pulled on his underpants, as if I had never seen him naked.

'Why don't you want to have children?' he asked.

'Does everyone have to want them?'

'No. But I do.'

Eerik had warm hands and sharp eyes. Against his body I fell asleep more quickly and woke more refreshed than I had ever been. Eerik wanted a child. I did not. I did not want to lose Eerik. Erik said he didn't want to lose me. I didn't want Eerik to be unhappy. Eerik said he wasn't, but he looked as if he was.

He touched me tentatively on the shoulder. I let his hand rest there although I wanted to push it away. Eerik drew a picture on my back. It was a long time before I realised that it was not a picture, but a poem, one that we both loved very much:

> I carry inside my heart,
> As in a chest too full to shut,
> All the places where I have been,
> All the ports at which I have called,
> All the sights I've seen through windows and
> portholes
> And from quarterdecks, dreaming,
> And all of this, which is so much, is nothing next to
> what I want.

'Do you mean I'm this easy?'

'I was being romantic.'

'You mean I should swap my pessary for Pessoa?'

Eerik laughed. I laughed. We made love, and that time we didn't argue about contraception. When, later, we lay side by side, my head on his collarbone, his hand caressed the warmth into my arm. Then I told him things that I had not told other people.

'When I was a child, my most important skill was to watch out for Mum,' I said to Eerik, and the movement of his finger brought warm ripples to the small of my back.

When I was a child, Mum was sometimes the most fun of all. She told me stories about the fairies who lived in the rose bushes in the back garden, made profiteroles with chocolate sauce for pudding, and let me try on the muff and golden shoes that she had worn when she was young. But everything could change very quickly. When Mum hid in her own world, a heavy curtain came down.

I learned to go to the shops and make food when Mum lay for long days in a darkened room listening to the music she had listened to when she was young. I learned to watch Mum's eyes. When they clouded over to dark olive, I learned to become invisible and to slip out, to steal sweets from the shops and give them to my friends so that they would invite me home for supper.

When I was in year nine, a new girl came to school. She had blue hair, a ring in her nose, and on the back of her leather jacket a peace symbol she had painted herself.

The girl's name was Nancy. In the first break three girls from another class in our year, who wore foundation that was too dark and stolen lipstick and who threatened everyone who was dressed in the wrong brand of jeans, beat her up in the loo.

I listened through the door of my cubicle as the girls pulled Nancy's hair. I lifted my feet up so that no one could see the toes of my shoes. I needed to sneeze, and I pressed my fingers to my nostrils so that there wouldn't be an explosion. There was a burning in my stomach. The same girls had once threatened to beat me up too, when my only Levis were dirty and I came to school in a skirt. Nancy had friendly eyes and badges on her jacket that said, *Animals Have Rights* and *War Against Apathy*.

It would be nice to talk to her, I thought when I saw Nancy for the first time. She was walking past the staff-room window and lit a cigarette. Now three girls were kicking her on the other side of the thin door, and I didn't go to help even though I could have done.

When the girls finally left, I pushed the loo door open cautiously. Nancy was adjusting her make-up in the mirror. Her nose was bleeding and one cheek was reddened, but she concentrated on outlining her eyes in black, smoothing her lips with cotton wool buds and drawing accurate line with lip liner.

'Nice, nice girls,' Nancy said in the mirror as she saw me come out of the loo.

'Yeah right,' I replied, and Nancy asked if I would like to borrow her eyeliner. I outlined my eyes to look like hers and we began to chat.

We talked about animal testing and the ozone layer and the unfair activities of multinational companies in the poorest countries. Nancy knew a lot, and I wanted to learn everything. We talked about how something in your chest tightens when you see the ships that sail to Germany or Poland and you think of getting on one of them, sailing across the sea to an unknown city and from there by train to somewhere you would never need to come back from. We talked about mothers and fathers and Sid and Nancy and punk rock artists like Pelle Miljoona, and Eppu Normaali and bands with names like Sunday School and Barren Virgin. Nancy was sure I would love them and promised to copy their records onto a cassette. When we talked, the air I breathed became lighter. It felt as if I had lived in a bubble until then and that Nancy had burst it with the point of her eyeliner pen. We bunked off school for the rest of the day and went to Nancy's to listen to music.

We lay side by side on the floor. A group called Treblinka played fast and loud; against my hand I felt the warmth of Nancy's arm. I imagined us hitch-hiking round Europe, playing in the streets of London, Paris and Amsterdam and doing *Something that would make everyone end this consumer party that's destroying the world!*, as I wrote in my dairy that evening, filling the margins with peace signs.

Through Nancy, I finally found a home. Nancy's friends became my family, and Mum didn't even notice when I left her to sleep with my new family in squats, to organise demonstrations against animal testing, nuclear power and the exploitation of developing countries and to hitch-hike to other towns to listen to bands at whose gigs we jumped hand in hand with people we didn't know.

After I got to know Nancy and her friends, my life was filled with an growing certainty that *something must be done*. Driven by that certainty, I left Mum and built a life in which I used all my time to make sure that something in the world would change. The idea of having a child did not belong in that life.

Why would anyone have a child in a world that is on the brink of destruction? I always thought when one of my friends told me she was pregnant.

'I daren't take responsibility for a creature that will be completely dependent on me,' I told Eerik. He had stopped drawing on my back and was listening to me quietly, his temple resting on his knuckles. 'What if I were to turn into my mother in the presence of a child? And what if the child couldn't get away from me?'

12

The first child was a girl. We gave her the names Aava Hilda Amanda. Hilda and Amanda, my maternal grandmother and Eerik's paternal grandmother, two women who worked from morning till night but never stopped smiling. And Aava for the open sea, which I loved and which I also taught Eerik to love.

When I think of Aava, this is the image that always comes to mind:

Aava is sleeping. The room is dim but not yet dark. Dust floats in the corners and from the garden comes the sound of a power saw. I sit beside her and pull the covers up over her ears so that the noise will not wake her, putting my finger beneath her nose to feel the warmth of her breath. I go to the door and come back to see that my baby is still breathing; I sit for a moment by the bed, in my limbs a heaviness that makes every movement difficult.

From now on, until the end of my life, I think, *my happiness is bound to the happiness of this person.*

Aava breathes a sleepy tickle onto my skin. I think about the children I have seen during the day, laughing and chatting in the tram but falling silent the moment a boy standing next to them tried to talk to them. When the boy eventually turned his head, his face was reflected in the window against the dark November evening. The smile frozen on his face was the same as all children who have to smile all the time.

The power saw falls silent. Aava screams in her sleep. I set my hand on her back. My hand is heavier than before.

13

Before my son was born, I thought I could not go on any longer. I felt strong contractions long before the due date; I lay on the sofa and tried not to cry. Aava ran around the flat destroying everything she could find. I ate chocolate in secret, letting her watch too much children's television. I closed my eyes and prayed that I might be able to call it all off.

We called the boy Lauri Aslak Eerikinpoika. Lauri and Aslak for our grandfathers, who went to war as young men and came back strangers. Eerikinpoika (Eerik's son) because I wanted to apologise to Eerik.

When Aslak was half a day old, Aava came to the hospital with Eerik's parents to visit him. Aava was three years and five months old; she had a woolly hat with strawberries on it, dungarees that sagged at the bottom and serious eyes.

Aslak was in Eerik's lap. I had read that it was good to do this when a child met its new brother or sister for the first time. It is good to give the baby to the father and it is good for the mother to take the firstborn in her arms. I was pale and broken from giving birth; I lay in bed and needed support to stand. When Eerik's mother rang to say they were on their way, I took a shower sitting on a stool, took off the pink hospital dressing gown and put on my own dress, dabbing some rouge on my cheeks, which were pale and yellowish from the blood I had lost. When the door of the family room opened and Aava came in holding hands with Eerik's mother, I walked unsteadily to take my child in my arms.

Aava did not want to come. She shrank back against Eerik's mother's legs and my mother-in-law lifted her into the air, whispering in her ear, 'Granny's here,' and promising her an ice cream in the hospital café when the visit was over.

On the other side of the room Eerik smiled, holding little Aslak, whose nappy he had changed and whom he had dressed in the hospital's white baby clothes and a hat that looked like an eggshell. While he did so I lay on my side on the bed, took some painkillers and closed my eyes, although I did not feel I could sleep.

Now I stood awkwardly at the end of the bed in a difficult position and looked at Eerik's mother walking with Aava in her arms towards her son and her grandson and Eerik's father followed them, a bunch of flowers in his hand, nodding to me as if asking forgiveness.

'Take a rest,' Eerik said. 'We can look after this.'

I took another painkiller, even though I should not really have done so, got into bed and tried to find a position in which the pain in my crotch and breasts was least unbearable, pulled the covers over my head and thought about a lone whale swimming in the Mediterranean, whose song the other whales did not understand.

14

'Mummy. Where does death come from?'

Aslak was four years old. It was a spring evening. The smell of fresh leaves wafted in through the window and the sky was pale even though it was late. Aava was on a sleepover with a friend and Eerik was in the Philippines redesigning a village that had been destroyed by floods. I was sitting on the sofa with Aslak, his soft cheek against my neck.

At that time there was something wrong with the radiators and it was always too hot at home. In the mornings when it was time to go to nursery Aslak would lie on the floor screaming and throwing his shoes, Eerik and I would take offence at everything the other said and Aava would sit in a corner somewhere, drawing quietly, and no one had time to ask her how she was. This moment with Aslak was full of peace and I did not want it to end, even though it was late. The light of the spring evening made a halo around his tousled hair. Aslak nestled in my arms and I stroked his bare arms; I wanted to paint a protective layer onto them.

We had been watching a movie in which wild rabbits fled from human habitation to look for a new home. In the film the rabbits are trapped, wounded and die. I hugged Aslak in my lap and asked him if he wanted to turn the movie off, but he shook his head vigorously.

'Does that happen to animals in real life?' he asked after the movie.

'We can try to make it so that it doesn't happen,' I replied after a long pause.

'But does that happen to them now?

'The same as in the movie?'

'Yes.'

'No. It doesn't happen to them quite like that.'

Aslak looked at me appraisingly, as if weighing up whether he could trust my answer. I remembered a time when my friends and I would go round shops that sold furs. At night we stuck pictures on the windows of mink and foxes in cramped cages, their gleaming eyes staring at the camera through the bars.

Even though we had not baked for a long time, for a moment the smell of freshly baked cardamom bread wafted through the room. I squeezed Aslak more tightly in my arms and felt the warmth from the oven as if I had a memory of a warm, fragrant home in which fresh cardamom bread was eaten on Saturday evenings. I thought about a time when Aslak and Aava would begin to think about the same questions I thought about when I was young, and how I would be able to talk about them with them. And their ideas would surprise me. My entire body overflowed with happiness. How amazing it was to hold in my arms a person who one day would step out into the world without me, challenging me with their ideas.

'Where does death come from?' Aslak asked again. 'Does it come from the mouth?'

I thought about my response for such a long time that Aslak pinched me to check that I was awake.

'It comes from life,' I said then. 'In the same way that night comes from day and day from night.'

'I don't want to die,' Aslak said. 'I only want to live.'

'You have plenty of time, sweetie,' I said. I tried to sound like a confident adult, the kind I longed for as a child.

'You will live a long life and do lots of exciting things. When you are old, you will be able to sigh contentedly and say that death can come now.'

Aslak looked at me dubiously. I told him about my granny, who climbed on the climbing frame in the playground so that you could see her lace petticoat. 'Granny died twenty-five years ago, but I think about her every day. So in that way she's still alive.'

We sat together on the sofa for so long that light gave way to darkness. Aslak wanted to know more about my granny, and I told him about the princesses of my childhood and the silver tray my granny gave me to be their skating rink.

When Aslak began to yawn, I carried him to bed. He was asleep before I put him in his bed, his face against my throat, his warm breath tickling my skin.

15

'I can't sleep.'

It was an August night. We were on a cycling trip in the archipelago. We were sleeping in a tent near the shore boulders, Eerik and I together in a large sleeping bag and Aava and Aslak in their own bags. An oil lamp hung from the roof of the tent and outside were our bikes, two little ones and two adult ones. As I looked at them something within me stirred.

We are a family. For some reason it was our belongings that brought that thought to my mind most clearly. Two pairs of little shoes and two pairs of big shoes in a row by the opening of the tent, two children's tickets and two adults' tickets to the circus, two little swimming costumes and two big ones hanging up to dry on the bathroom rail.

When I was with Eerik, Aava and Aslak, I was often restless and nervous, mechanically performing the tasks that went with the roles of wife and mother and longing for a moment when none of them would demand anything of me. I felt the deepest love for them when I was alone, tidying things or folding clothes. As I made the beds, I would pause for a moment to breathe in the scent of the children's pyjamas; as I filled the dishwasher I decided to wash by hand the elephant mug Aslak had used since he was one. He had refused to give it up, even though he would be going to school in September. Those years were so full of work, my own and the children's interests, money worries and increasingly panicky questions about what I would be able to do with my life, what was I good enough for or whether I was good enough for anything, that there was most room for love when my loved ones were absent. Love was at its strongest in moments when I was able to pause alone to cherish images of them, images that lacked the imperfections of real people.

Aslak's little hand stroked my cheek from a slit in his sleeping bag. His fingers were warm, his voice a whisper that did not wake anyone else.

At that time I did not sleep very well. Generally being woken at night annoyed me, but now I could hear the roar of the waves on the other side of the tent canvas, and from the opening of the tent wafted the smell of the sea.

'Shall we go and look at the stars?' I asked.

'Yes!' Aslak said, with such enthusiasm that I was struck by guilt. Why didn't I make such suggestions more often? Why didn't I ask my child to come with me more often, since my invitation brought him such joy?

I switched on the torch and looked in the darkness for our sweaters, windcheaters and shoes. We had made pancakes for supper and I packed the ones we hadn't eaten, sprinkled with sugar, in a box. I took this with us, and a quilt. Grasping Aslak's hand, I slipped out through the tent opening. In the wind that caressed our faces was the coolness of the autumn that was to come; the waves pounded the rocks with an even crash. The sound always calmed me. The sky was clear, and a bone-white full moon bathed the stones in a pale glow.

I spread the quilt on the stones and we sat next to each other on it. Aslak curled up in a little ball in my arms; I could feel the bones of his shoulders under his sweater and smelled the scent of sleep and the campfire in his tousled hair. We made rolls out of the pancakes and ate them with our fingers, listening to the sea and the chirping of the grasshoppers, which Aslak could hear much more clearly than I could.

'Mummy,' Aslak whispered. We had been sitting for so long that I thought he had fallen asleep in my arms.

'What, love?'

'What's it like to be a grown-up?'

'Why do you ask?'

'Because I don't know.'

I was amused, but Aslak was completely serious. I hid my laughter with a cough giving Aslak the last pancake.

'It depends who you ask. It's probably different for everyone.'

'What's it like for you?'

'Different. Rushed. Sometimes stressful. Mostly, it's nice.'

'Is it nicer than being a child?'

'For me, yes.'

'Why?'

'When I was a child, there were so many questions that I didn't dare ask. When you're a grown-up, it's easier to look for answers.'

Aslak lowered his head into my lap and asked me to draw a spaceship on his back. He had loved his back being drawn on since he was very small; it had calmed him as a baby and as a toddler and when he had nightmares and screamed, his eyes open even though he was asleep. With my forefinger, I drew a spaceship standing on a launch platform, its sides swelling on either side of Aslak's spine. I wondered when it would be time for me to tell him and Aava something about my childhood.

Aslak and Aava met Eerik's parents often. I told them about my mother only when they asked about her, and often after those conversations I wanted to be alone. I wondered whether Aava and Aslak would fail to understand themselves fully if I never told them about anything but beautiful moments. If I didn't tell them about how, as a child, I had pressed my ear against my front door and listened for a long time before I dared open it, how I had carried a secret that no one was allowed to know.

Aslak shifted in my arms. The night was cool and his warmth spread to me.

'I think it's nice being a child,' he said softly, as if he were already falling asleep. 'But I don't want time to pass.'

'Why?'

'Because then one day it will end,' he said, and his shoulders trembled a little.

'Our own time ends,' I said, 'but the Earth's life goes on. I think that's a beautiful idea.'

'Why?'

'Think of the sea, for example,' I said. 'The sea has been here for billions of years before us. And it will still be here when we no longer exist.'

'I want to live for ever,' Aslak said, turning his head so that he could see the sky. 'I want to see all the countries in the world and all the stars in the sky. I want to learn all the languages and stroke all the dogs in the world.'

'I'll draw them on your back.'

'All the world's dogs, can you? Will they fit?'

'I'll draw them one by one.'

Aslak curled up in my lap so that my hand could reach his back better. I slid my finger under his sweater and drew dogs – pointed-eared ones, floppy-eared ones, long-haired and almost hairless ones – until his body flinched into sleep and his lower lip stuck out as it always did when he slept.

I carried Aslak back into the tent, put him in his sleeping bag and kissed his smooth cheek. After that I went out again, walking on the stones until the sky began to lighten. I concentrated on every sound, every snap under my feet, every scent that came from the sea and the interior of the island.

16

Aava

'You take these white ones.'
'No, I want the pink ones!'
'OK. You can have the pink wings, but I'm having the pink wand.'

I was nine and Aslak six years old. We thought we were too old to play games like this and so we played them secretly, in the playroom with the curtains shut, behind a closed door. The darkened room became a fairy world in which we two superfairies were able to read minds, see through the walls of the neighbours' house and make others do our will.

We were AA-superfairies. We were able to fly through walls, become invisible, breathe in outer space and under the water. I was a day fairy. I had a pale skirt and flowers on my cheeks and I knew how to spread light into the darkest corners. Aslak was a desert fox. He had transparent wings on his back, and on his temples fox ears that could hear everything; around his eyes the dark rims of fox eyes. Aslak the desert fox used the cover of darkness to find maltreated animals, free them and take them to a secret refuge where he looked after them until they were better and gave them magical powers that they could use to fight against humans.

At that time Aslak often asked me to play with him, but I seldom said yes. I was at school and I had my own friends whom I used to go home with after after-school club. Aslak was in the same nursery school as the siblings of some of my friends and I knew that the others thought him strange. He learned to read and write when he was three years old and sometimes beat Dad at chess. But when the other children asked him to play with them, he often got lost in a world of his own, staring at a shadow that moved on the wall or at something behind it, and then, after a long silence, saying something that no one else understood. I hoped that a year would change something in him. That when he came to school he would be a more ordinary boy, one whom no one laughed at. I wanted to think that I hoped this above all for his sake, so that it would be easier for him to fit in. But really I hoped it mostly for my own sake. I was afraid that if everyone else thought my little brother was odd, I too would be left alone.

When we did play together, we generally played superfairies. I too longed for that world when there had been an argument with my friends or Mum and Dad spoke to each other in voices that were supposed to sound normal, but which I knew would explode into an argument in the evening when they thought we were asleep.

'AA-superfairies, check all areas!'

'AA-superfairies, roger!'

Aslak was no longer a little boy, but a loose-limbed, sharp-eared, all-powerful desert fox fairy. He looked under the beds and on the bookshelves, inspected the cupboards, the little holes in the walls and the world that opened up on the other side of the window.

'A fire engine!'

'Water fairies! Fire!'

'For real!'

'What?'

'Silly. There's a real fire engine by the garden!'

'Wait!'

'Come on!'

When Aslak came through the door, he was no longer a fox, but an ordinary little brother, smudges of face paint around his eyes, on his back pink fairy wings, his eyes glowing with excitement on account of the fire engine.

Mum was out shopping and I would have liked to have gone on playing. It felt strange. The room was half ordinary playroom, half fairy kingdom. I was half ordinary Aava, half fairy-tale creature. All of a sudden the feeling that I was somewhere in between was unbearable.

When I took the white wings off my back and put them carefully back in the dressing-up box so that the fine fabric would not tear, it was as if something were ending. My hands shook as I closed the lid. At the same time I was closing the lid on something else. I had always thought the fairyland was our hiding place, my and Aslak's shared world, which we could escape to whenever we wanted to. Now I realised that our fairyland could disappear completely and that I would not be able to go there even if I wanted to. My tummy hurt as if I had eaten too much cake mixture. I went to the toilet and sat on the loo for a long time without turning the lights on. When I came out, I found pencils and a piece of paper and began to draw a map of fairyland, so exact and detailed that I would be able to find my way back there when I had grown up. When Mum's key turned in the lock, I had barely begun.

'Where is Aslak?'

'He went out.'

'But I asked you to look after him.'

'There's a fire engine outside. He went to look at it.'

The fire engine was still there, but there was no sign of Aslak. I went with Mum and we walked round the garden, the fire engine and the neighbouring streets. Mum picked up her phone and I wondered whom she should call. The lump of dough in my tummy grew so large that I couldn't swallow.

'How could you leave him alone like that?'

'I didn't think he would be so stupid.'

'Aslak isn't stupid, just little.'

'He's going to school next year.'

'He's still little.'

'I'm little too!'

I burst into tears. Mum didn't hug me; she didn't even stroke my cheek. She looked at me angrily, and for a moment I thought she was going to hit me. She looked up the numbers of Aslak's nursery school friends' mothers and wondered whom to call first, how she could summon up the nerve to ring any of them and say she had no idea where her child was. I wondered what nerve had to do with something like this, but didn't dare ask. Shame thickened around us like air that was too hot. I didn't understand what was shameful about the situation but I did know that it was all my fault.

Mum breathed heavily, speaking in a shrill voice. The phone in her hand vibrated. As I looked at it, my legs and arms went limp like spaghetti that has boiled too long.

Up till then I had believed that grown-ups had a big secret. That grown-ups knew for sure how to be in the world and what you should do when. Dad and Mum were often tired and got angry easily; sometimes I was woken by Mum's crying. All the same, I believed that beneath all that grown-ups had a strong and steady core, an inner stability that nothing could completely destroy.

'We will make sure that nothing bad will happen to you,' Mum and Dad repeated when I or Aslak was scared of something – riding a bike, swimming, going to a birthday party, getting run over by a car, fatal illnesses or playing the piano in the music academy concert.

'We will take care of you.' I had believed it. I had believed that grown-ups had a secret way of making the world good for children. Now, looking at Mum's shaking hands, I understood that this was not so. Grown-ups were just as scared, just as helpless, as children.

I wiped my tears on the sleeve of my blouse and looked at the familiar buildings, the familiar hedges and streets on which I had learned to ride a scooter and a bike, to skip and to twist and to hide if a child I didn't want to play with came out. Everything looked the same as before, yet everything had changed. Playing and running in these streets I had always thought that I was safe, that someone was looking after me. Now the wind blew on my face more harshly than before, the sounds of the cars were sharper, there was a threat in the faces of passers-by. On the path up to our front door hopped a crippled sparrow. The bird pecked at some bread that had fallen to the ground, flitting away when someone approached it.

The someone had bare feet. There were bruises on his legs, his trousers and shirt were torn, a scrap of pink tulle clung to his collar, his face paint had run from under his eyes onto his cheeks. Mum dropped her phone and ran to Aslak.

'Darling. What happened?'

Once inside, Aslak said nothing. His mouth was a narrow line and his eyes, lined with black face paint, were dark pools. Mum took off Aslak's dirty clothes, discovering that the back of his shirt was torn and his skin was raw and bloody. Aslak stared at the floor and scratched one ankle with the toes of his other foot.

I went to the bathroom to fetch some antiseptic wash, some cotton wool and plasters for Mum. I stood on the toilet seat to reach the medicine cupboard and saw in the mirror a face that was very pale, and much older than before. At my back I felt a light wind, as if someone had walked quickly by.

'This is your fault,' said a voice inside my head. It was Aslak's voice, Mum's voice, my own voice. And the voice of someone else, a stranger who was staring at me, someone who could see everything and knew what would happen to a badly behaved girl.

When I went back to Aslak and Mum, my steps were heavier than before. I would have liked to become very small, to curl up in Mum's arms and cry, to let Mum stroke my cheek and say everything would be all right. But Mum spoke only to Aslak.

'Darling. You need to tell us what happened,' Mum repeated, but Aslak said nothing, just looked at the floor and scratched his feet. For a moment I thought Aslak was perhaps somewhere completely different, on a sun-warmed shore boulder by the sea. That he had left us and would never come back again.

17

Laura

Y ou think life will be a certain way. You think
that however difficult it is, the most important
things will always stay the same. You know you belong
to a privileged group, small but permanent. Then the
world changes. And only when it is too late do you
realise that everything really is possible. It is possible that everything you have considered certain will
be swept away. It is possible that one day we too will
flee war.

I wrote that in my journal when Aslak was seven
and Aava ten years old. The Iraq war had been going
on for years, and I could not get it out of my thoughts.
I thought about children who saw their parents die,
who hid when soldiers in heavy boots came to get their
father. I thought about the closed shops, schools and
hospitals, the people who left their homes, quickly
packing their most important belongings, setting out
without knowing where they were going.

I thought about my young granny, in her shiny shoes and white coat, saying goodbye at the railway station to the man whose child was making her belly swell. Granny put a note in her husband's coat pocket, saying she was knitting him a scarf, she would go on knitting until the war ended; the scarf would have blue-and-white stripes and would be as long as the war. *When the wool slips through my fingers, I will think of your skin*, Granny wrote, not knowing that she would never wrap the scarf around her husband's neck, would never finish the scarf.

She would bring up the girl in her belly alone, would work three shifts and carry the unfinished scarf in her bag from one small flat to the next. In the evenings her daughter would sit on the windowsill waiting for her mother to come home, pressing her nose against the glass, not daring to go back into the room, which was cold and full of ghosts.

I wonder what we would do if a war really did begin. Where would we try to go?

That same year, Aslak started school. On his first day I took the day off work and we walked to school together. Aslak was wearing his new yellow jeans and a yellow T-shirt with a racing-car print. He had chosen his clothes himself, comparing different combinations and looking at himself in the mirror for a long time in a way that made Eerik uncomfortable, even if he did not say so. Aslak walked beside me but would not hold my hand. His face was unsmiling and his gaze sombre; his hair, the colour of an unripe strawberry, glowed in the sun.

A little before the school gate, Aslak stopped.

'What's up?' I asked.

Aslak kicked the ground with the toe of his tennis shoe and gestured towards the school gate with his hand. Children were walking to school like ants executing a task. Pairs of girls in glittery sweaters, whispering, heads together; groups of boys on skateboards and scooters; bigger children greeting each other easily and the big, confident nursery-school children who had, over the summer, been transformed into small, shy first-formers, toting brand new backpacks, shoulder to shoulder with a friend.

I saw what Aslak had seen: everyone else had a friend. Everyone else was coming to the first day at school with someone else, the bigger children with a group of friends and the first-formers with dense groups of adults and children, family friends together. Only Aslak and I were alone together. No one was waiting for him at the gate and no one would walk with him to the classroom.

I crouched down in front of Aslak and stroked his cheek.

'Are you feeling nervous?'

He kicked the ground, biting his lip in the same way as Eerik did, then shook his head.

'You can go,' he said. 'I'll be OK.'

The skin of his cheek was as soft as a kitten, his voice brave. I clenched my teeth and looked at a seagull that was tugging at a pizza box in the rubbish bin.

'I'll come and collect you,' I said. 'We'll go for an ice cream.'

'OK,' Aslak whispered, his voice trembling with suppressed tears. An icy pain spread from my stomach towards my neck. I pressed Aslak quickly to me; his heart was beating like a shrew's, his breathing tickled my neck.

'Have a lovely day, sweetie.'

Aslak did not reply. He waved quickly and set off, head and shoulders stooped as if expecting a beating, towards school. I rushed home swallowing my tears; it was only when I reached my own front door that I realised that I had forgotten my bag.

'He will be fine,' Eerik said when I called him, weeping so much that at first he could not make out what I was saying. 'We have to believe that he will be fine.'

18

'Mum, can I come with you?' Aslak was eleven years old. His eyes were serious and his face narrower than before; his limbs were longer and everything about him seemed suddenly to have become darker and sharper than before, his body and mind awkwardly uncertain at the point when a child is growing into a teenager.

I was on my way to an Open University course to talk about the same subject as always, climate change. Eerik was in his study, Aava out with her friends, and Aslak was in his room playing computer games, as he did every evening in those days. As I packed my bag in the hall, Aslak appeared beside me as if from nowhere, his phone in his hand, wearing pyjama trousers and a T-shirt. He looked at once small and big, and I had to hug him close; to my amazement he stayed still for a moment.

'Why do you want to come?'

Aslak shrugged his shoulders.

'There's nothing to do.'

I stroked his cheek, covered with soft down.

'I'd like to hear what you say,' he said finally, with forced cheerfulness.

'Really?'

'Maybe.'

I hugged him again. His shoulder blades rose under the thin shirt like wing stumps.

'Do come with me, sweetie. It would be really nice.'

Aslak put on jeans and sneakers, I kissed Eerik goodbye, and Aslak and I fetched our bikes from the back garden, cycling through the August evening to the darkening city.

At that time the family was strange to me. Eerik and I were in a polite but distant phase; neither of us had the energy to build bridges. Aava went round to friends' houses after school or shut herself in her room with them. When I tried to talk to her, her short responses made me feel absolutely ancient. Aslak spent his evenings in his room behind closed doors. Sometimes I knocked on his door, sitting on the edge of his bed for a moment and asking him questions to which he did not respond. As for me, I had the time and space for which I had yearned when the children were small, but the gloomy silence that hovered over our home was so suffocating that I was tired from morning till night.

Is that all there is to life? I thought, remembering me and Eerik when we were young, full of a thirst for each other and for the whole world. Ordinary life and a surreptitiously deepening strangeness, was that all that lay in store for us?

When Aslak cycled ahead of me through the city with its smell of high summer, my pedals moved more easily than for a long time. I looked at my son's tousled hair, which had grown long, and the narrow back revealed by his fluttering shirt. I remembered how, when he was two, he used to be wakened by nightmares, how I bent to stroke him, how he used to squeeze his fingers firmly around my forefinger.

'This is my boss,' I said to the people who had come to listen to my lecture. I ruffled Aslak's hair and felt an overwhelming desire to keep him close to me, to find a language in which I could get him to talk to me.

'Pleased to meet you!' everyone said to Aslak, and Aslak responded with an embarrassed smile. Amid the well-dressed, thoughtful adults, my son suddenly looked different from before, relaxed and adaptable. He took his computer out of his backpack and sat next to a lanky young man to listen to me.

'We talk about the climate crisis but continue to live as if there were no crisis,' I said at the beginning of my lecture, and Aslak looked over his computer at me intently and sharply.

'At the same time the climate crisis influences how we treat one another,' I said. I cited research according to which global warming and the associated change in rainfall increase violence both between individuals and between large groups of people. Aslak's eyes looked like coins darkened by age.

'If we cannot control climate change, by 2050 the risk of violent conflict will have grown by fifty per cent across the globe. Do we want to leave our children such a world?'

To finish, I quoted the French philosopher Michel Serres, whose writings give form to things that are difficult to understand.

'According to Serres, humanity is for the first time in a situation in which we can have a effect on the entire globe. Our impact reaches the entire globe and out into space,' I said.

'When we lived in an agrarian society, we learned to live at the mercy of nature, which was strong and governed life. Now we leave traces on the environment which we encounter everywhere. There is no escape. Our imprint has made nature fragile, its power uncertain. Nature can mend itself only when it has space to do so. Now humankind has become a parasite which takes all the space away from nature. To stop it, our only option is to make a contract with nature, as Serres suggests, to find once again a way to live in harmony with nature.'

Aslak looked at me quizzically, whispering something to the man next to him and tapping some notes with quick fingers. His forehead wrinkled and his ears stuck out beneath his long hair – he had suffered from their size since he was small. For a moment I saw an image of him as an adult, with a smart suit and serious eyes, talking about the same subject to different audiences, calling his listeners to action in a world in which there would be much more hope than now. I closed my eyes so that the image would linger for as long as possible.

I was in the habit of dreaming constantly of alternative worlds, conjuring up pictures of me, Aava and Aslak in strange landscapes and new stories. The pictures coloured new layers into life, suggesting that life was not merely a succession of ordinary days, one after another. That somewhere there was also something else, another time, another life and another kind of self; that there was still something to come. But now I realised that I had not imagined anything about Aslak for a long time. I had seen nothing but the present moment, endlessly continued, and a boy whose life I watched powerlessly from afar, in which nothing would change. Perhaps it was precisely this that was the cause of the gloominess that hovered over our flat like dust that gathers in corners.

After the lecture, I stayed to talk to the students. Aslak came up to me and to my eyes he looked for a moment like one of them, a gifted, enthusiastic boy for whom the world was an open book. I did not want to go home.

I wanted the evening with Aslak to go on unhurriedly. I asked if he would like to have something to eat with me and was startled when he said yes.

We cycled to a café where Eerik and I used to go before we had children, drinking wine and gazing at the ice-cream-white surface of the cathedral. Years ago the café had meant limitless time, the chance to order glass after glass of wine, milky coffee and little pies which were served on porcelain plates. There Eerik and I had talked about the past and the future, about our fears and dreams and, on summer evenings, moved out into the courtyard to watch movies, wrapped together in a blanket, going with the movie to Tunisia, Italy or France, looking at people who walked in high-heeled shoes on the cobbled streets. The things that happened in their lives were carefree even when they were sad, melancholy even when they were carefree.

The table Eerik and I used to sit at was free. Aslak sat down opposite me and set his backpack down on the windowsill; I moved it onto the floor underneath the table. Aslak glanced at me with irritation, but neither of us said anything. I ordered chocolate cake and tea for both of us. I would have liked a glass of wine, but it was important to have the same as Aslak. His relaxed demeanour at the lecture had disappeared. The veil that had seemed for a moment to have lifted had come down again. He spooned up his piece of cake with lowered head and responded to my questions in short sentences. I did what I always do when I am ill at ease: filled the space with trifling talk, which made Aslak withdraw even more.

'Who do you spend time with at break time?' I asked, regretting my words the very moment they came out of my mouth.

'No one,' Aslak said, and his face was reflected, long and pale, in the surface of his plate.

'Is it horrible?'

'I think it's quite OK to be alone,' he said with a smile.

I felt the smile as a sharp stab beneath the skin of my belly. It was my smile. The same smile that I pulled across my face as a child like a mask on the warm mornings when I wore a long-sleeved shirt to school to hide the bruises on my arms. It was the smile that I pulled across my face when I said I couldn't come to gym class because I had a tummy ache. And when I told the teacher, the school psychologist and my friends' parents that everything was just fine, absolutely fine.

Aslak let me grasp his hand. His hand was thin, but the skin was still soft and childlike; he did not squeeze my hand back, but neither did he pull it away.

'You are a lovely, clever and sensitive boy.'

'Mum. Please don't.'

'It was nice that you came with me. Will you come again?'

'Maybe.'

'You can come whenever you want.'

19

I was sitting in the corridor of the parliament building, waiting for the door to open and for it to be
my turn to go inside. I was on my way to talk about
reducing emissions to the members of parliament,
some of whom always looked as if they were not in
the least interested in the matter, while others asked
pointed questions which had nothing to do with what
I was talking about. Even though I had been doing this
for a long time, I always felt uncomfortable in these
situations. I was wearing my one and only suit and
a pair of black boots whose worn tips revealed that
I did not look after my shoes regularly, if at all. I have
never understood how people who look after their
shoes, their skin, their body, their hair, their wool-
lens or their household appliances according to the
rules ever have time to do anything interesting, such
as work, read books or meet friends. Even though
I had reached the age when one is addressed formally
in restaurants, in official situations I always felt like a
young person dressed up as an adult, a black-haired

girl living in squats who had charmed a boy with beautiful eyes by pushing a safety pin through her cheek when drunk.

I gazed at the austere walls of the parliament building, mentally running through the most important things I wanted to say to the members of parliament.

'The scientific community has long been, for all practical purposes, unanimous that emissions caused by the human race are changing the climate.'

'It is no longer the time to talk about whether this is happening. We need to talk about what to do about it.

'If we do not begin reducing emissions now, everything will be much more difficult in future.'

Alongside these sentences, phrases of a different kind moved through my mind:

'We cannot go on like this.'

'You are perfect in every way, but we cannot go on meeting like this.'

'I can't bear it for a moment longer. I will say I am on a business trip and come to you.'

He was half Danish and half Egyptian. He had wiry hair and cheeks red from cycling, and he was much younger than me. I met him for the first time at the Montreal climate conference. After that he came to a couple of seminars to listen to my lectures, and a little later to my room for the night.

I had never thought I could cheat on Eerik. Even though we were often tired, frustrated and bored with each other, Eerik was the first person with whom I felt at home. When he touched me, Eerik was, even after years of living together, polite and a little clumsy. I often thought about other kinds of men, faceless and powerful, whose hands would not ask but would decide what to do, undo the buttons of my blouse and turn me towards the wall. At the same time I loved Eerik for the very fact that his hands moved softly, struggling with shame.

Eerik and I had been distant from one another for the entire time that Aava and Aslak were little. At that time I felt that another life existed alongside my own life, the one which ended when I was pregnant with Aava. In that life I loved other men and women besides Eerik, travelled around the world, read books endlessly and was an outsider everywhere in a way that wasn't distressing but liberating. Very often, as I encouraged the children to get dressed in the morning or brush their teeth in the evening, as I sat in parent–teacher meetings, answered messages from teachers or folded laundry in the evenings, it felt as if someone were watching me.

That someone was a woman who had not met Eerik or given in to his wish to have children. Much as I loved the children, I would hardly have become a mother if Eerik hadn't had such a strong desire to be a father.

The decisions we make are hardly ever clear or unconditional. Rather, we drift into them, making decisions that will turn our lives upside down or change their direction completely. How often are decisions to get married or divorced, to try to have children or not to try, to leave a job, change or end one's life, made in the grip of absolute certainty, without a tremor of doubt that it might be possible to act another way?

Eerik does not think like this. He believes his choices are always clear; he weighs things up and then makes his decision, and once he has done so, he does not doubt it. For Eerik, becoming a father was a dream come true; for me, becoming a mother was a choice which I never completely ceased to question. I never completely shook off the feeling that a me who had made a different choice was watching my life. Often there was something condescending in that gaze, something deeply pitying.

When the wiry-haired man grasped my hand under the table in that Montreal bar, everything that had until then seemed inevitable changed. I woke up. The body which had for decades made do with getting enough sleep and exercise, and some gentle tenderness, began to demand decisive, long-lasting caresses which would make me forget everything else. When the man came with me to the door of my room, it was clear that I would let him in.

My phone vibrated in my handbag. Aslak.

'Mum. Can Taika come round?'

'Who is Taika?'

'A new friend.'

I forgot the man. I forgot the members of parliament waiting on the other side of the sturdy door, who would soon be asking me in. I forgot the November rain beyond the window, and the darkness, which each year became longer, deeper and harder to bear. The usually shady corridor was now full of light, my uncomfortable suit, soft as a cloud.

Aslak was in fifth year at school and this was the first time he had wanted to ask a friend home. Aava went to friends' houses after school or brought them home; when I arrived after work there could be many pairs of silver or glittery shoes in the hallway, many brightly coloured coats. Aava's door would be closed and from her room would come the sound of music, giggling and girlish voices as they stood in front of the mirror singing their favourite pieces, microphones in hand, or taking pictures of each other in which they looked up sideways, their hair mussed and their cheeks sucked in. No one came to see Aslak. He did fencing for a while, and played the cello for many years, going to rehearsals alone by tram, with his instrument in its black case on his back, his eyes hidden by his hair, which he wished would cover his entire face.

'Of course, sweetie!' I answered. I would have liked to go home straight away. I would have liked to see how my little boy behaved with his new friend. What was he like, this first friend whom my Aslak wanted to invite home? What was Aslak like in his company, what were they together? I wanted to go home via the shop, to buy food that all children liked, to make pancakes for supper and do it as if it were absolutely ordinary, as if Aslak had a friend over every day and I cooked their favourite foods, as if I really were that kind of mother.

The heavy door opened. A short, constantly smiling member of parliament in a well-cut suit stood on the threshold.

'Laura Anttila?'

'Pleased to meet you.' The words flew from my mouth, light and airy, like butterflies spreading their transparent wings.

I rose to my feet and shook the member of parliament by the hand. As I stepped into the large room, the sun shone even though the sky was covered in clouds.

20

'Mum, look what we did!' Aslak's hair was tousled and his cheeks were rosy with enthusiasm. He had grown, and his legs looked too long and thin for the rest of his body, his nose and ears too big for his head. Taika stood behind him, examining me furtively. Ever since Aslak had asked her home for the first time, they had been together every day. All the same, Taika was still shy in my presence, as if she were constantly afraid she would make a mistake. Taika's father was Finnish and her mother Japanese. Her hair, which reached beyond her chin, was as black and shiny as a grand piano, her cheekbones sharp as wings, and her dark eyes narrowed to streaks when she laughed. She had lived in Kyoto for three years and entered Aslak's class in the middle of the year, walked up to Aslak in the playground and asked: 'Where can I find the best books?'

Aslak had taken Taika to the school library, and after school to our library and to the second-hand bookshops whose smell, ceiling-high bookshelves and sharp-eyed booksellers, who knew everything about books, he had loved from the time when I had taken him and Aava there to listen to stories. Aslak and Taika had borrowed comics, children's novels about sorcerers and alternative worlds and non-fiction books about outer space, coming home to eat avocado sandwiches which I had left for them in the fridge, and spent the entire afternoon lying on Aslak's bed, reading books and comics side by side, laughing when one read their book aloud.

Taika arrived in our lives so naturally that it felt as if she had always been there. When I bought tickets for the family for the theatre or the winter circus, I bought one for Taika too. In the morning as I set out for work I left a sandwich in the fridge for her too, and after work I made supper for five. Taika was a vegetarian, like Aslak, me and Eerik. I bought silken tofu from the Japanese shop for her; I filled maki rolls with avocado and cucumber and made soup from tomatoes, chickpeas and saffron. Aslak and Taika sat side by side to eat. They talked with me and Eerik at the table but I was sure that they were simultaneously engaged in another conversation, communicating with each other wordlessly about things we were not allowed to know.

At that time Aava was always quiet at table. She looked at the food I had prepared, turning up her nose, so clearly that I definitely saw it, but so fleetingly that I could imagine I was mistaken. She was in ninth year and ashamed of all of us. She wanted a mother with shiny high heels and a carefully made-up face and a father who wore a suit instead of worn-out jumpers. She wanted a brother who played football or went skateboarding and not one whose only friend at school was a nervously giggling girl. She wanted to go to her after-school classes by car, to holiday in the Canary Islands and eat meat for supper.

I felt that Aava's sulkiness was justified. Her periods had started and her breasts had grown a little. She used deodorant which she had bought herself and covered her spots in concealer every morning. She shut herself in her room for hours and did not meet her friends as often as before. It was her age, I told myself. I had always thought of Aava like this. She might shout, slam doors and cry, but there was something strong and clear about her. She had friends and hobbies, she laughed her head off at her own jokes and spoke up bravely against me, Eerik and her teachers. Everything about her was strong and understandable. She would rebel, hate us and might even reject us for a while, but her difficult phases would pass without breaking her; she would change, grow and manage without us.

I had always been worried about Aslak. You could see straight away from Aava's eyes what mood she was in; Aslak's eyes showed nothing. Aslak was like a dense bolt of gossamer-fine fabric that would disintegrate if you tried to open it. He had many layers, one within the next, the outer one a withdrawn boy who had learned to be well-behaved, and beneath it something that no one could see.

When the children were small, I thought it would be possible to keep them close. Eerik and I talked a lot about the importance of always remembering to listen to the children. We should know them so well that we would recognise the gestures with which they tried to hide their sorrows. In those days I thought that everything depended on how sensitive we were able to be, how open to their needs, how close to them. As Aava and Aslak grew, they became independent from us in completely different ways. Aava was often openly angry, slamming the door of her room shut, spending a lot of time away from home and wanting to be different from me in every way. Aslak was polite to us, and heartrendingly good. He didn't go anywhere, but submerged himself in his own world. It was as if an enormous blue expanse opened up within him; when he dived into it, he could see neither the surface nor the sea bottom.

I moved away from my mother's house when I was fifteen, but I thought that I was an exception. I thought children only left bad parents, that good parents could keep them close. When I struggled with the children over getting dressed, brushing their teeth or going to bed, I dreamed of a time when we could make food with them, light the candles and talk about anything and everything. I saw visions of two energetic young people who had grown taller than me, who would bring their friends round to our house and go to the cinema or to listen to music with me and Eerik. I thought of me and Eerik, our hair grown grey, talking over a *caffè latte* or a glass of port about our grown-up children whose joys we could still share and whose problems we would be able to solve.

When Aava and Aslak fled from me, each in their own direction, I was taken aback and numb. I could not speak of my grief even to Eerik. Eerik went on long trips and buried himself in his work. He chatted to the children about school and about his work. Sometimes after a sleepless night I waited for a moment when I could tell Eerik what I was thinking, ask him to come to me and smile until everything was all right. He never came.

'Don't start again,' he said when he saw my eyes, begging like those of an anxious child. 'Everything is fine with Aava and Aslak. They're not you. You're not your mother. Give them space to live.'

And gradually, although I did not think of it in that way at the time, I gave up. I let them go. I accepted the distance that had become permanent, and concentrated on what I did best – work.

Aslak still had faded scars under his shoulders, a memory of the day when he went to look at the fire engine with his fairy wings on his back. Despite endless entreaties from me and Eerik, Aslak never told us what happened on that day. He hid it inside himself like everything else; sometimes when I looked at him, I could almost see a black hole in his chest from which nothing could escape.

I was embarrassingly enthusiastic about Aslak and Taika's friendship.

'Aslak is in a completely new phase,' I explained to my friends, whom I had earlier told about my concerns about him, always in an artificially light tone.

'Time has done its work, just as you said,' I explained.

'Of course I should have trusted that everything would work out. But when you're in the middle of it all, and when it's your own child, you only see the worst outcomes.' In fact I was constantly on my toes. My lonely boy's sudden, intense friendship felt as if a rare flower had been brought into our home, one which I must keep alive.

'Lighten up,' Eerik said. 'Leave them be.'

Now Aslak and Taika were standing in front of me, glowing with enthusiasm. In Aslak's hand was the video camera Eerik's parents had given him as a Christmas present.

'Look!'

Aslak gave the camera to me.

'It's at the beginning, you can watch it.'

I opened up the little screen and pressed the play button. A light shining onto the wall of Aslak's darkened room cast an unearthly glow on the face of a person standing in the middle of the room. That person was Aslak. He was dressed in black trousers and a tight black shirt; he had painted his face white and drawn clown-like lines around his eyes, a clown's tear on his illuminated face.

'Hi, I'm Niko,' he said, drawing out his vowels in a way that brought to mind one of his classmates, a boy who was taller than all the rest.

'I play footie and I'm wicked at it, I always get the ball into the goal when no one is guarding it. It's just a pity that once the ball hit me on the forehead and destroyed what little brain was left. And now . . . and now . . . and now . . . zzxxbbaaghszgh . . .' In the video Aslak fell onto the floor and remained motionless. The camera zoomed in to the tear drawn on his cheek, whose outlines had blurred a little.

Aslak took the camera from me. His hands were warm.

'That is our first movie,' he said almost in a whisper.

'We're going to make movies like that about everyone in our class.'

Taika said nothing. She looked at me, the same enquiring expression on her face as always, as if she had seen the horror spreading within me.

'It's ... it's ... it's ...' I said. Expectation quivered on Aslak's face. The wrong words would crush him. 'You're really good at using the camera.'

I smiled as naturally as I could. I turned to empty the dishwasher so as not to have to look at them.

21

The relationship with the man with wiry hair continued for two years. When I was with him, the part of me which I had shut away when I chose Eerik, motherhood and family awakened. The skin that the man's hands touched did not belong to Eerik's wife and Aava and Aslak's mother, but to the independent woman whose eyes had followed me for years. That woman met the man at the stations of Berlin, Rome and Madrid, kissed the man in unknown streets, drank wine in bars where everyone else was younger than her, lay naked with the man in the early hours of the morning and made love once more as the rising sun cast its tender light into the hotel room.

With that man I did not think about Eerik or the children. I had left the door ajar to another world, an alternative reality and another kind of life. The man stood on the other side of the door, ready to take me to him.

When I was with Eerik and the children, I thought about that man. There were always two women with

him. One belonged in their lives; the other had continued her life without them. I knew that what I was
doing was wrong. I was distant with the children and
irritable with Eerik. When we got married, we had
agreed that we would be honest with one another.

'I will understand if at some stage you fall in love
with someone else,' Eerik said, 'but I want to be the
first to know.'

Kind, decent, honourable Eerik. He saw a clear line
between right and wrong and did not understand why
everyone didn't stay on the side of what was right. He
would have despised me if he had known. He would
probably have hidden his pain, borne it alone and tried
to behave in such a way that no one would be hurt.

Those years were heavy with guilt. At the same time
they were the lightest years of all, full of the tenderness of long caresses and the joy of being desired. I
knew it would not last for ever; that was why I wanted
to hold on to it. Telling Eerik would have made what
was beautiful ugly, would have turned joy to immense
sorrow. There would have been a trial, with my secret
as the crime.

'How long? How many times? Where? What? How?
Were you together that time when you said . . .? And
that the time? And that time when you came home
from a trip and lay with me and . . .?'

That is what Eerik would have asked, and I could
not have answered. It would have gone on so long that

everything would have been dug up, and once on show it would all have been ugly.

For all of that time I loved Eerik. But I also felt that I was not completely his. Part of me had chosen him and the family; part was still hesitating. That part belonged only to me and, for that period of two years, to the man who saw me differently from the others.

One evening during those years, when I was sitting in the kitchen reading and thought everyone else was already asleep, Aava came to me. She was barefoot, in a white nightdress; the light from the street lamp through the window cast a transparent glow onto the fabric. Aava walked so softly that it felt as if she had landed beside me from another world.

'Mum,' she whispered, and her voice startled me.

'Sweetie. Why aren't you asleep?'

'I can't sleep.'

'Why?'

'I'm frightened.'

'What of?'

'That you're going to leave us all.'

Aava was taller than me. I grasped her by the hands and took her in my arms on the sofa like a child. She pressed her head against my neck and curled up her legs, her long, slim Bambi legs, which at that time she used to try and hide beneath long, floaty skirts.

I stroked her back and calmed her as I used to when she and Aslak were little, by drawing dense forests on either side of her backbone.

'Sweetie. Of course I won't leave you. Why are you afraid of something like that?'

'It's just that it sometimes seems ... as if you'd rather be anywhere but with us.'

My finger halted next to Aava's backbone. She had lost weight; her vertebrae rose beneath the skin in a sharp row. I looked through a slit in the Venetian blinds and saw the single woman in the house opposite opening the window and lighting a cigarette, stretching her hand out and waving it in the air as if to see how it felt. I could not look at Aava.

'Oh, darling,' I said quietly. I could not find the words to go on. Shame spread through me like icy water.

How ridiculous I had been. How could I have imagined that they would not see? That the children, who see and sense everything and carry it quietly with them, wordlessly protecting their parents and what they imagine to be their family, how could I have imagined that they would not notice what was happening to me?

I drew on Aava's back for so long that she fell asleep; then I picked her up. She had long arms and legs, which dragged along the ground as I carried her. She weighed so much that I almost fell, but I felt it was my job to carry her to bed.

Aava did not wake when I tucked her in, stroking her hair away from her forehead and switching on the fairy night light which she had had since she was a baby.

When I left Aava's room, I heard a crash from Aslak's room. I pushed the door open cautiously. The window was open. A spring night breeze and the scent of newly emerged leaves flooded into the room, with their promise of something good. Aslak's quilt was at the foot of the bed, his pillow on the floor beside the bed.

I switched on the light. The curtain twitched. Beneath it I caught a glimpse of the soles of Aslak's feet. I thought he might be sleepwalking. I walked up behind him softly, tentatively touching him on the shoulder through the curtain.

'Sweetie?'

'Go away.'

'What's wrong?'

'I want to be alone.'

Aslak was twelve years old, but I could hear the seriousness of a grown man in his voice. I stroked his back cautiously. He was so thin that his shoulder blades stuck out like sharp wings. Something about him brought to my mind the monkeys that I saw years ago in a Nepalese zoo, wild-eyed creatures sitting quietly in their cages, their bones sticking out through their matted fur. Next to him on the table was a red droplet. I wiped it away with the sleeve of my blouse. When I realised what it was, I tore at the curtain with such force that the curtain rail and the curtain fell onto Aslak.

'Leave me alone!' In Aslak's right hand was a flick knife. I had not seen it before. On the inner side of his forearm were fresh, long gashes.

I recognised the gashes immediately. On my wrists, on my thighs and on my ribcage I still have faint scars from the time when I cut myself with the shards of a hand mirror I had smashed while my mother was asleep. I still remember the moment of relief that flashed through me, when the vague, surging angst was replaced by a pain defined by the length of the cut. I grasped Aslak by the hand and took the flick knife away. He did not resist. The flick knife was an old one. The wooden handle was worn, the brass at the end tarnished. There was dry blood on the blade.

'Where did you get this?' I asked, biting my tongue.

'Nowhere.'

'I'm sorry.'

I sat on the table beside Aslak. He let me put my arms around his shoulders and stroke his hair, which was wet with sweat.

'My sweetie,' I said. 'What has happened?'

Aslak was silent. His head rested against my neck. He was breathing lightly like a frightened animal; as I stroked his back I felt the rapid beating of his heart. When he finally spoke, at first I could not hear what he said.

'Taika is leaving,' he said finally, loud and clear, in the voice of a stranger. My hand was still for a moment. I breathed in. *We will get through this*, I thought. *I must get Aslak to believe it.*

'How long for?'

'For ever.'

'Where's she going?'

'Japan.'

'We can go and visit her there,' I said quickly. 'Although not this summer. You can get there by train and ship if you go through Russia. It would be fun!

'Everything will be all right, sweetie,' I went on when Aslak did not say anything. 'It really will.'

'I'm tired,' he said at last.

I tucked him in, and he allowed me to stroke his head until he fell asleep. He was a narrow-shouldered, big-eared boy with a child's face who looked as if he was in the wrong place. As he slept his face smoothed into that of a young child; his long eyelashes cast feather-like shadows on his cheeks. I remembered the time when he was always laughing, when he made everyone around him laugh.

Eerik did not wake up when I finally lay down beside him. He was sleeping on his back, his mouth slightly open. There was a trail of dried drool at the corner of his mouth and he was snoring fitfully; I could never get to sleep while I listened to it, and tonight was no different. I sat beside Eerik, looking at the moonlight shining through the gap in the curtains, cautiously stroking his hand. For a moment I felt again the gaze of the self that lived a different life. It was no longer full of pity, but pure grief. When, in the early hours of the morning, I fell asleep, I dreamed a dream in which she went away without looking back, and after that I never felt her presence again.

22

Aava

'Can we come to yours after school?'
        'Could we go somewhere else?
'Why?'
'We're always at my house.'
'So what? You've said we can come to yours.'
'It's different now.'
'What do you mean?'
'It's just . . . we've got a situation.'
'What?'
'I can't say.'
'Aren't we friends?'
'Yes, but . . .'
'No?'
'Of course we are.'
'Why can't you say? Don't you trust us?'
'I do, but . . .'
'You don't seem to.'
'It's not to do with me.'

'What do you mean it's not to do with you?'

'Have you got an illegal immigrant in the cupboard?'

'The word is undocumented.'

'What?'

'Undocumented, not illegal.'

'Oh, for fuck's sake.'

'Well, do you have an undocumented immigrant?'

'They could have. Her mum takes food to the gypsies.'

'I get it. It'll be her brother.'

My diaphragm tautened, the same way as once in football when I was goalie and the ball hit me straight in the stomach.

'Is it? Aslak's gone crazy?'

'No, he hasn't.'

'I bet he has.'

I shook my head. I curled my hands into fists and thought about the trip to Copenhagen in the summer and the Swedish boy who had kissed me on the lawn of the outdoor swimming pool. The boy had broad, soft lips and his mouth tasted of strawberry chewing gum and beer. '*Du är så vacker!*' ('You are so beautiful!'), the boy said in Swedish, opening the beer; we drank from the same bottle and sat with our sun-cream-scented legs touching.

I was fifteen. It was vital to act as if everything was fine.

'Sorry. I'm not feeling well.'

I sprinted away. I ran over the boulders where I had picnicked with Aslak and Dad as a child, along the little paths to the shore where some of the boats were still in the water even though the autumn was well advanced. I looked at the boats floating in the dark water; one wooden one was half sunk, its outboard motor completely beneath the surface. For a moment I felt like turning to see whether the water could be pumped out of it, whether the beautifully made craft could still be raised to the surface. I was wearing high-top shoes and tight jeans. As I ran my jeans chafed at my ankles and the seams rubbed my thighs. I wanted the pain to go on, for the skin to be scoured until it bled.

After Taika went back to Japan, Aslak did not come out of his room. He stayed up all night playing games whose names he did not tell me. During the day he kept his curtains drawn, lying on his bed with his face to the wall and did not touch the food that Mum brought him.

At that time we all stayed awake at night. I read *The Hunger Games* in bed, wrote in my journal and listened to Mum and Dad talking on the other side of the wall.

'You should talk to him,' Mum said.

'He doesn't want to talk,' Dad said.

'How do you know?'

'You can see.'

'You don't even try.'

'I don't think it's necessary at the moment.'

'What is, then?' Mum's voice rose to a shout.

'We have to give him time.' Dad's voice tightened to the official tone he adopted when he was angry.

'We have to get him help.'

'It's hard to help someone who doesn't want help.'

'He's twelve. You can't ask him what he wants.'

'What do you want to do? Send him to an institution?'

'You're the one who doesn't want to do anything!'

'Oh, is that what the problem is?'

'What?'

'The fact that you think I'm not doing enough.'

'Did I say so?'

'It sounded as if you think—'

'Don't you try to bloody guess what I'm thinking. Say what you'd do.'

'I would leave him in peace.'

'That's all you ever do.'

'His best friend has just left. It's a difficult age.'

'He's always been difficult.'

'So you say. But he's always been good at school. He hasn't been in trouble. He's a good boy.'

'He hasn't had a single friend for years.'

'He just had one.'

'The only one.'

'People don't all have to be the same. You often say that. That the limits of normality have shrunk too much. Now you're shrinking them yourself.'

'He's my son.'

'Don't shout.'

'Don't shout yourself. Our son is sinking and you behave like some fucking official.'

'Don't swear.'

'Fuck off.'

I tried to become invisible.

'I will give everything up,' I promised God, the forest spirits, the angels and the demons; I promised the same thing to every imaginable power.

'I will give up everything I have if you will let Aslak be happy one day. I will give up my friends, my hobbies, music, books, happy days and long evenings. I will give up my health, my dreams and my life. Let Aslak be loved and me be alone. Let Aslak live and me die.'

When nothing changed, I asked: 'Let Aslak die and me live. Let Aslak disappear from the world so that he never existed. Let me be the only child and let me breathe freely, even for a short time.'

Aslak did not leave his room. In the end Mum bought a car and drove him to school every morning, waking him by playing music, feeding him breakfast like a little child.

I, too, wanted to sink into eternal rest. I went for a long run before school every morning and ate so little that my clothes became baggy. I drank a lot, passing out at parties, on beaches and at festivals, waking in the arms of strange men, pushing them away and running, except that I did not always have the energy to run. I hoped that something so bad would happen to me that Mum and Dad would be forced to see me. I stole lipsticks, underwear, cigarettes and jewellery. Once I was caught and I was happy, thinking that for once the responsibility rested with someone else and that Mum, who would come to collect me from the brightly lit back room of the department store with the stocky security man, would be forced to see the whole of me.

'How could you do something so stupid,' said Mum, pushing me in front of her like a child.

'Don't you realise how worried we are about Aslak? Why do you have to behave like that, too?'

23

Beautiful death. Private group.
Someoneisoutthere:
Hi. Where have you disappeared to?
Someoneisoutthere:
I'm worried.
Someoneisoutthere:
Send me a message, let me know you're alive. I'm
    going to call the cops soon!
Übermensch:
You and the cops. I bet.
Someoneisoutthere:
What's happened?
Übermensch:
Nothing.
Someoneisoutthere:
What did we agree?
Übermensch:
To be honest with each other. Do you mean to say
    you always have been?

Someoneisoutthere:

You know the answer. I wouldn't be alive without you.

Übermensch:

I'm not sure it's worth anyone's while.

Someoneisoutthere:

That's a different question. You said no one can survive in the dark alone. Do not try alone.

Someoneisoutthere:

Did you disappear again?

Übermensch:

Wait a minute. I'm going to send you something.

Übermensch:

Here.

ASLAK ANTTILA. YOU ARE A FUCKING STUPID
QUEER. YOU LOOK STUPID. YOU SPEAK STU-
PID. YOU HAVE STUPID CLOTHES. YOU TRY TO
BE COOL AND LICK THE TEACHERS' ARSES,
BUT EVERYONE CAN SEE YOU'RE TRYING TOO
HARD, YOU ARE A FUCKING STUPID QUEER
AND YOU WILL NEVER BE ANYTHING ELSE.
NO ONE LIKES YOU AND NO ONE WILL EVER
LIKE YOU AND THAT'S WHY YOU SHOULD TOP
YOURSELF BEFORE IT'S TOO LATE.

UNKIND REGARDS

All the pupils of 9A, 9B, 9C and 9D.

(EXCEPT FOR IIRIS, WHO'S A LESBIAN
WHORE!)

Someoneisoutthere:
Idiots.
Someoneisoutthere:
Are you still there?
Someoneisoutthere:
Hello . . .?
Übermensch:
What if they're right?
Someoneisoutthere:
They're not.
Übermensch:
They'd be happy if I died.
Someoneisoutthere:
They're morons. Who cares what makes them
   happy?
Übermensch:
What sense is there in living?
Someoneisoutthere:
Go to the window.
Übermensch:
What?
Someoneisoutthere:
Just go.
Übermensch:
You're crazy.
Someoneisoutthere:
What can you see?

Übermensch:

The street. The street lamp. The building opposite. Trees.
Some old lady taking her dog out for a walk.

Someoneisoutthere:

Look up.

Übermensch:

Stars. The moon.

Someoneisoutthere:

I can see it too.

Übermensch:

Are you playing at being Coelho or something?

Someoneisoutthere:

Fuck off.

Übermensch:

OK. We're looking at the same moon. So what?

Someoneisoutthere:

I couldn't look at it alone. I couldn't bear it if you
weren't there. You have to live. You have to laugh
at the idiots who know nothing. You're the only
person in this world who gets me.

Übermensch:

Coelho!

Someoneisoutthere:

If I was there, I'd beat you up.

Übermensch:

Sorry.

Someoneisoutthere:

Do I have to spell it out? You're important.

Someoneisoutthere:
If you disappear now, I'll never forgive you!
Übermensch:
I won't disappear.
Someoneisoutthere:
Do you feel better?
Übermensch:
A bit.
Übermensch:
Thank you.

PART
THREE

A thousand dreams within me softly burn.

ARTHUR RIMBAUD
Oraison du soir
('Evening Prayer')

24

The city

It is a foggy, damp night. Mist softens the outlines of the buildings; the light of the shops and the street lamps pierce the darkness like white, yellow and red stars. Trams, buses and trains appear as if from another world; there is the gleam of lights and a moment when people move from cold to warm, warm to cold, avoiding one another's eyes. The fog condenses into droplets on the steps of the parliament building; before them a group of Egyptian refugees set their phones to silent and bow towards Mecca. The smell of cooking aubergines rises from a portable grill and a sheet fluttering in the wind bears the legend, *We Too Are People*, in Arabic and Finnish.

A young member of parliament runs past the refugees, umbrella in hand; the wind catches his bobble hat, which lands in the midst of the prayerful group. Bareheaded, the member of parliament steps into a taxi.

Close to the refugees, under an unemptied rubbish bin, two ducks sleep side by side, like brindled stones. The Egyptians have kept camp in the same place for three weeks, and every evening after prayer the ducks get up and ruffle their feathers, the people stretch their limbs and finish making their supper, offering the left-overs to the ducks. The wind ruffles hair and feathers and they eat together in silence, people and ducks, in a tight ring in which the close contact gives warmth to everyone. But tonight this does not happen.

On a quiet train a young woman reads a collection by a poet who stuck her head in an oven a long time ago and thinks about the moment when she will step under a train, her coat open and in her pocket a book that was written for her.

But soon the trains stop running, and the woman ends up far from the deserted platform, on a rock damp with rime. She is gazing at the empty Ferris wheel when a young man sits down next to her. In his bag is a saxophone and in his mind the same poems. The woman and the man sit on the rock until the sky grows light, listening to the sleep-silent city in which everything is different for a moment. When they make love, it is on the cold rock and with their clothes on, and only later in the man's studio flat, on the bed and the floor in a warm room, and many times in many places inside and outside, until they no longer make love but talk to each other until the man gets married and the woman moves to another country and the connection is broken.

The woman lives to be older than any member of her family before her, reads new poems in new places and, on happy mornings, thanks the man who sat on the rock beside her, and the other on whose account the city grew silent.

The couple, who have spent three decades together, leave their coats at the theatre cloakroom. The woman helps the man to take off his coat, as has been their habit ever since their first date. What began as a protest against gender stereotyping continued as a tender act after the man fell from a ladder while mending the summer house roof and hit his shoulder on a rock; after the operation his arm no longer moved in the same way as before. They were going to watch a play about the battle of the generations and the sexes, power, loneliness and the need for intimacy. They saw the play together for the first time more than ten years ago when the children were going through a calm phase and the whole of life was so full and peaceful that it felt as if they were on a long holiday. The man's mother looked after the children, and after the theatre they went to the park to drink champagne, watch the trains and dream of how, in retirement, they would tour the world.

Now new cancer cells have been found in the woman's lungs and she has decided to cease treatment and live, as long as she has life, enjoying the thoughts of the people she loves, reading books and listening to music, gazing at beloved landscapes, spending relaxed days with the man whose touch, even after three decades together, is still an adventure.

They are going to the theatre because the woman wants to see a new version of the play which, the first time she saw it, troubled her for months. She wants to breathe in the smell of the old theatre and think how many people breathed it before she was born, how many will breathe it after she has died.

When the performance is interrupted, people leave the theatre fearfully in a horde, seeking news, asking each other for information. The man and woman take a detour home and follow the news on the sofa on which they kissed and made love and got their children to sleep. They imagine the empty centre of the city and the man standing alone on the roof of the white building, and neither of them thinks about how many months the woman still has to live.

A man, who as a child dreamed of a career as a turtle researcher, pulls a wheeled cart towards a building whose cellar exhales warm air and along whose walls homeless people sleep on cold nights. There is a laceration on the man's nose and blood flows from the corner of one eye; there are crumbs from a hamburger he found at the tram stop in his beard, and in the supermarket trolley a floral quilt which a young women threw onto a skip after her mother's death. The man is waiting for the moment when he can pull the quilt over him and close his eyes, feel the warm air blowing on his back and sink for a moment into a sleep as quiet as death. But the man is directed away like everyone else, and far away from the centre someone gives him a disposable cup and some hot coffee; it warms his insides in a way no one who sleeps indoors can understand and, for a moment, as he tastes the coffee and listens to the shocked, horrified, disorientated people, the man feels himself to be one of them.

A mother and daughter, both of them adults, come out of the cinema together. The evening was the daughter's idea. She is forty and her mother seventy. The daughter is weary of the fact that when they talk together they both regress to childhood, so their conversations have become short and rapid, and after them they both feel uncomfortable.

The daughter was divorced two years ago from a man who was, according to her mother, too good for her, and now she goes to therapy twice a week. She talks to the therapist much more about her mother than about her husband. The previous winter the mother fell and broke her hip, and since then the daughter has felt that the mother may die at any time. The daughter suggested the evening at the cinema because she wishes to learn to talk rationally with her mother before she loses her.

For many years the daughter hoped that one day they would have a big, cathartic conversation. That they would talk about the things that come between them whenever they meet. About why the daughter, who at work stands in front of hundreds of people making complicated things clear and understandable, becomes an anxious child when she is with her mother. She hoped that they could talk, listen and understand one another so that they could leave childhood behind. Now all she hopes is that they can meet every now and then and talk about something ordinary and unimportant without every sentence containing an insult. They do not have to understand one another. They do not have to talk about anything important. Nothing needs to be cleansed. But she hopes that before her mother dies she might be able to meet her without being distressed for days afterwards. That is why they are now walking out of the cinema, and the daughter is suggesting that they should go somewhere for a glass of wine.

'I saw a programme where they said that women your age drink too much wine . . .' the mother begins, but the sentence is never finished.

The mother presses her hands to her ears and the daughter falls to the ground clutching her shoulder, which is welling up with blood.

25

It is quiet. If the police sirens are sounding, he cannot hear them. The blue flashing lights look like indistinct pictures, soft-edged images from videos shot in unknown cities which make the city more a state of consciousness than a place, a sea of lights dancing in the darkness. The atmosphere is recognisable, even if the place is not.

The damp air is easy to breathe. He squeezes the cool butt of the rifle and feels himself slipping into his own place in the world. This is the place he has always been looking for. It is sad that he can enjoy it only for a moment, but good that he has found it now.

He closes his eyes, stroking the rifle like a cat curled up in his lap, presses the weapon against his shoulder, puts his forefinger on the trigger and aims again.

26

Laura

The policemen wait silently as I walk towards then. In the high entrance hall of the university they look out of place in their uniforms, a tall, bald man and a woman with a bob, perhaps my own age, on their faces carefully practised neutral expressions.

'Laura Anttila,' I say, reaching out my hand.

'Lauri Aslak Anttila's mother?'

'A young man has shot four people from the roof of the Glass Palace.'

'The police suspect that the gunman is your son.'

'We would like to ask you a few questions.'

'You have the right not to answer them.'

'We can go to the police station or to your home.'

I raise my fist to my mouth and bite the knuckles hard so that my teeth leave marks.

'Home. My husband will soon be back from a business trip. Supper is in the oven.'

I gaze at the street through the police car window as if from inside an aquarium. The policewoman drives and the tall man sits beside her in silence. The silence is broken by the sirens of approaching police cars.

As a child I stood on the side of this street with my grandmother waiting for the Christmas lights to go on. As an adult I wanted to bring Aava and Aslak here every year to see the Christmas lights being switched on. Even as a grown-up, there was a fairy-tale magic about the lights being switched on above the street in the midst of the end-of-year darkness, as if the lights shone from somewhere where it was always light. We stood in the crowd, Aava on Eerik's shoulders and Aslak on mine, the children holding warm roasted chestnuts in paper bags, Eerik's arm around my waist. When the lights were switched on and the procession of elves, angels and snowmen went past us as the music played, there rose to my eyes tears of joy, sorrow and longing which I was unable to explain to Eerik.

For the rest of my life, as I remember this evening, the first thing I remember is something that I tell no one. It is the feeling that something that has long been in disarray has been put in order. A lost jigsaw puzzle piece has been found, a bottle stopper that fits perfectly, an artist whom the public has been expecting to flourish for years suddenly succeeds.

I never speak of this feeling to anyone, not even Eerik. The reason is shame. The certainty that this feeling is unquestionably and irrevocably wrong. Parents have a generally accepted right to be concerned for their children only when the child plays the role of victim. Every parent recognises the constant fear that something bad will happen to their own child. The tightening of a band around the heart when you see your child standing in the playground apart from the others and the weight in your stomach when it is late and your child has not come home.

When a quiet pupil comes to school with a weapon under his long coat and shoots ten of his classmates, everyone is supposed to think about the victims' parents. How awful it would be to be one of them. How awful it would be if that happened to a child of mine. You can talk about fear and anxiety to others because everyone recognises this. Parents who forget to breathe when reading such news because they know that the shooter could be their child bear their horror alone.

27

In their uniforms, the police officers look amazingly large; their presence fills the entire room. The smell of long-braised swede wafts through the kitchen. If you were to slash the skin open, you could sink a spoon into the interior as if it were baby food. I open the oven door and mistakenly grab the roasting tin with my bare hands; the hot pan burns suppurating, blistered lines into the palms of my hands.

I wet two towels with cold water and wrap them around my hands. The floor sways and vomit forces its way up my throat. It must not come now, not when there are others here.

If only Eerik were behind me, not the police officers. If only Aslak were coming round for supper. If, in a few moments, he were to be standing at the door, looking around him as if he had been followed, and we were to conduct, in the hall, our complicated, embarrassed ritual: Welcome, sweetie, how nice to see you, switching places to hang Aslak's coat on the hook. If only we were to hide the wine bottle and offer him juice, slip the kitchen knives quickly into the corner of a high cupboard and put the beautifully arranged starters on the table; if only I were to exchange glances with Eerik, uncertain when would be a suitable moment to say what we intended to say this evening.

'Sweetie, there are people who can help you,' I would say.

'That's what you always say,' Aslak would reply without raising his eyes from his food, which he would be cutting clumsily and decisively, as if executing a motor-skills test. 'But no one can.'

'Care methods are developing,' I would say. 'There are various therapies, various *methods*, various *projects*, which are designed to help young people just like you.'

'I'm not young,' Aslak would say. 'And I don't want help. There's no need.'

I would spit my food into my napkin and get up to clear the table in order to avoid his gaze.

I would turn on the tap, sink my hands into the warm water and start washing the dishes by hand instead of putting them into the dishwasher. I would be angry with Eerik, *Why the hell don't you say anything?* I would imagine the moment after Aslak's departure, how I would throw a plate on the floor and shout at Eerik, this was supposed to be a joint project; Eerik would slam his fists onto the table, his neck red with fury, *How could I say anything when you were spewing those idiotic clichés the whole time that make Aslak angry, what could I have said?*

'You have nearly the whole of your life ahead of you,' I would say to Aslak. 'You have the opportunity to do all sorts of things. If you will only let us . . . if you will only accept help.'

'All you want to do is get rid of me,' Aslak would say in his grating voice, scraping his knife across his plate in a way that gives me goose pimples. 'You just want me to be someone else's responsibility.'

I would cut the swede into slices and fry them in butter until they were soft and caramelised. I would carry the barley risotto to the table and burn my fingers on the rim of the saucepan, running them under cold water for so long that I no longer felt the pain. I would change the subject.

'Can you go on?'

The policewoman touches me lightly on the shoulder.

'I can.'

'It would be very helpful if you could answer a few questions. You also have the right to remain silent. It is possible that your answers may be used in court against your son.'

I turn on the tap and rinse my face with cool water. The water runs beneath my collar, under my bra. Generally cold water makes me feel better; today it just makes me wet.

'I will answer all your questions.'

28

Aslak is standing in front of me. In the wide-angle lens he is fully visible, behind him a tidy and impersonal room. Aslak is wearing a black wind cheater, black trousers and trainers that I bought him. In his hands he is squeezing a long, narrow object. When I understand what it is, I press my head into my hands even though I have decided to cope with everything I have to cope with this evening.

My arm is too heavy to lift, my lungs are constricted, my throat feels blocked; I cannot swallow. The room is still filled with the smell of swede, even though I have just scraped the remains of the soft root vegetable into the bin. If I open my mouth, I will be sick.

'Are you sure you can do this?' asks the policewoman.

For a moment there is another room before me.

It is spring, and I am eighteen years old. My matriculation exams are just beginning; I'm spending my reading week in the Rikhardinkatu Library. I spend my nights sometimes on the floor of a squat, sometimes in my old room, avoiding my mother. In the library reading room, sitting at a dark wood table, among other silent people bent over their books, it is hard for me to concentrate on my studies. In front of me is a text about history; my thoughts hover over future images. In these images I am far away from everything I know. I hike, rucksack on my back, in the Himalayas; I am sleeping in a hammock on a Brazilian beach; I am naked, riding a horse, into the sea. The images go with me as I pack my books into my backpack, close the library door and walk towards my childhood home, towards my mother's kingdom, which I will soon be able to leave behind for ever. Through those images, the familiar streets, parks, buildings and tram stops change. This is a city I can leave.

After school, I go to work in a shop that sells tourists from Japan and the United States plastic reindeer, Lapp hats and glass jars decorated with Finnish flags. They are labelled 'Finnish Reindeer Droppings' and contain reindeer poo arranged on tufts of moss. I buy clothes from the flea market, eat porridge, potatoes and fried herring, and save most of my wages. Sometimes, in the evenings, I leaf through my bank book in which the recorded balance rises steadily, each zero full of possibilities. After my exams I begin to sell the same things at the market; I have agreed to long days and weekends, while in the evenings I have promised to paint Father Christmases and snowflakes on the jars in which the reindeer poop is packed.

I have calculated that eight months of long working days and thrifty living will be enough. After that I will be able to pack my rucksack and take the cheapest flight, Aeroflot via Moscow, to Delhi. If I live in the cheapest youth hostels and travel second class on the train, my savings will last for six months. I can travel through India and Nepal or change my plans and go to Thailand, Laos or Vietnam. After six months I will be able to look for work wherever I am or somewhere else. I can work and save, and when I have enough money, I can set off again.

The air is heavy with thunder, but as I walk towards home my steps are light. Not much time to go now. Reading week, the exams, the certificate which will allow me later to apply to university here or elsewhere, to find new people and new ideas, a new place for myself. One last effort, and I will be free.

At my front door the smell greets me like a quilt thrown in my face. I know immediately where it is coming from. Even before I go into my bedroom, still wearing my shoes, my backpack on my back and my T-shirt, damp with rain, like a cold bandage against my stomach, I know where it is coming from. Even before I see my mother on the bedspread wearing a lace nightdress and dramatic make-up (who did she think would find her?), I know where it is coming from. I also know, before I lift the receiver, that the phone bill has not been paid. I open the window, brush my tousled hair, rinse the faint traces of tears from my eyes and ring the neighbours' doorbells, first our floor and then the next, and when the old man on the top floor finally opens his door, I explain the situation calmly and without my voice trembling; I am equally steady when I explain it to the emergency operator and to the doctor in the ambulance that takes my mother to the hospital.

When my home is finally empty, I wash the bed-spread and the sheets, pack pencils, rubbers, rulers and food for the next day, carry my mattress out to the balcony because I cannot sleep inside and there are too many people at the squat, gaze at the stars and try to get to sleep. The following day I go to school in good time, put on my headphones in the language class and concentrate on listening to the Swedish oral test. When, in the middle of the exam, I begin to feel faint, the invigilator takes me out into the corridor and asks me how I am feeling. 'Fine,' I reply, smiling so radiantly, so sincerely and for such a long time that there is no way she can ask more.

I open my eyes.

'I can,' I say to the policewoman. 'Go ahead.'

Aslak walks closer to the camera. The lens distorts his face. For a moment he comes so close that his eyes look too far apart, his mouth too wide and thin. He takes a step backwards, brushes his hair from his eyes, takes from his pocket with a dramatic gesture a letter written on transparent paper and begins.

'To the world,' he reads. '"Do you believe that a good intention sanctifies even war? I say to you: a good war sanctifies everything."' Aslak pauses and looks straight at the camera. I grip the sides of the chair.

'Thus proclaimed the philosopher Nietzsche almost 150 years ago. His words are repeated by those of us who have begun the war against humanity.' Aslak pauses again. He has washed his hair and combed it back. The scars left by spots are visible on his forehead; his pale face is narrower than before.

'Have you heard a cuckoo singing on the shore of a quiet lake? Have you skied in a snowy forest and seen the trees bending with the weight of snow? Have you seen a giraffe spreading its legs and bending its long neck to drink?'

I press my hands against my chin. I think about my heart, its valves, its arteries and chambers, an organ the size of a clenched fist, pumping blood until it stops. 'Do you know it? The beauty which is so pure that it is impossible for us to understand it. The beauty which is almost impossible to find because we are everywhere met by our own traces.'

Aslak's voice is trembling. As if he were moved by his own words.

'In June this year the population of the globe exceeded eight billion. There are more people than ever before, even though we have long known that there are too many of us. We are a parasite which is trampling beneath it the living space of all other species. *Homo consumericus*, man, whose only goal in life is to consume and take pictures of itself consuming, has become a monster. It is necessary to destroy the monster.'

Aslak raises his hands and places the tips of his fingers together, as if he were giving a political speech. He could just as well throw boiling water in my face.

'As long ago as the end of the last millennium the philosopher Michel Serres demanded that we should make a contract with nature – at the risk of our own survival. We did not—'

The image paused. I paused it.

'What's wrong?' asks the policewoman.

I shake my head. I rewind and listen again.

'As long ago as the end of the last millennium the philosopher Michel Serres demanded that we should make a contract with nature – at the risk of our own survival. We did not make a contract. We multiplied and peopled the globe. We are a heavy slab that crushes everything else beneath it. We must yield.'

The room in front of me becomes fragmented. I attempt to turn my head. It will not turn. The policewoman places her hand on mine.

'Shall we pause it?'

'No.' I say that. My mouth functions. My hand can move again.

'Until now, those people who have the most money have prospered.' Aslak pauses. From the screen, he looks me straight in the eye. He has the face of a child.

'The only equitable way of choosing who may live is chance. Do not choose your victims. Get weapons and kill those who cross your path. Do it quickly and effectively, avoiding unnecessary suffering. We are not cruel. We do not derive enjoyment from violence. We do not do this to cause destruction, but to save Planet Earth. We invite every responsible individual to join us. When time runs out, all that remains is a burden that no one can carry.'

Aslak walks out of the picture. The camera shows an empty, ascetically tidy room. From somewhere comes music, gradually becoming louder: 'Nobody Home'.

29

Aava

'Madam, is everything OK?'

The guard has walked up behind me quietly. He is young, almost just a boy; the sleeves of his uniform are too short and a rusty Kalashnikov hangs from his shoulder. I set my porcelain cup down on the ground and smile at him.

The man's name is Bahdoon, he who keeps care of the clan. When Bahdoon is on evening shift, we talk from time to time. He has taught me some Somali and asked me to teach him English.

'I want to follow the international news,' Bahdoon explained, 'so that I know what people are thinking elsewhere. I want to at least imagine that I have some connection to a world that is quite unlike this.' In the evenings I have seen him standing by the wall, his rifle at his hip, looking at the mould-decorated wall as if he could see through it.

I have learned Somali to be able to chat with the guards and the cooks and, on field trips, to be able to talk to the children who look at me as if I had come down to earth from a fairy tale. There may be perils in the villages, but when I work there, I generally feel at ease, able to be of at least some help to others. Here, I constantly feel uncomfortable. It is difficult to have natural conversations with local people when you live on a small island guarded by watchtowers and go to work wearing a bulletproof vest and helmet. Every encounter is charged with the unspoken knowledge that while we are in principle equal, as all people are in principle, nothing in our lives will even distantly resemble this.

Now I want to run away. I wonder how to say so without insulting Bahdoon. He is looking at me as if my skin were transparent.

'You look sad, sister.'

I smile. A bone-hard, forced smile: I can do this well. I have always loathed crying in public. The fact that someone makes themselves the focus of a sad situation and demands that other people react to it. When I was younger, I looked down on my sixth-form classmates who sobbed that they were ugly and fat (and went from one boy to the next to hear that they were really thin and beautiful) and on my student friend who fainted during an exam after her boyfriend had left her and whose well-being was a general cause of concern long afterwards, as if heartbreak was something exceptional that happens only to extraordinary people. At that time Aslak kept to his room, taking medicines that made his fingers swell and his speech thick. My entire social life was based on hiding the pain associated with Aslak. It is for that reason that I hate crying in public. Public expressions of sorrow are possible only if the grief that gives rise to them is sufficiently insignificant and ordinary, something that can be told to everyone without any isolating shame.

'Everything is just fine,' I say. The corner of my hut is visible through the branches of the trees. The room is cold at night and hot by day, and all the sounds of the garden can be heard. But the doors and windows can be closed, the lights can be switched off and the covers can be pulled up; under the covers you can turn on the bright light of an e-reader. Bahdoon walks quietly beside me, the barrel of the rifle swaying against his hip. He hangs his head as if he need a pat; the neck that rises from beneath his shirt could belong to an old man.

'What about you?' I ask. 'Is everything OK with you?' Bahdoon looks at me as if he has been expecting the question for a long time.

'Did you hear about the attack?'

'Which one?'

'Al-Shabaab, the hotel. Thirty dead journalists.'

'Everyone's talking about it.'

'My best childhood friend died in it.'

Bahdoon stops so suddenly that I nearly bump into him. He looks fragile and delicate; the wind could blow him away.

'I am terribly sorry.'

Bahdoon rocks on his heels, fiddling with a dry blade of grass. His fingers are long and beautiful. I imagine what they would look like fingering a violin in a European concert hall, in warm light, in front of a perfumed audience dressed in rustling clothes.

'Did he work in that hotel?' I ask. I regret it immediately.

'He killed the workers.'

'Oh. I'm—'

'He was a member of al-Shabaab.'

'. . . sorry.'

We walk past my quarters and continue to the other side of the yard. The noise from the bar, the chirping of crickets, the pounding of the waves and the gunshots from the town sound soft, as if someone had wrapped everything in gauze.

'When we were children, we used play pirates and al-Shabaab fighters,' Bahdoon says. 'There were a lot of us – me, him, his brothers and the neighbours' children.' I imagined what the town must have been like then. How the smell of food cooked on charcoal would have mixed with the reek of burning car tyres and the voices of ibises, pigeons and storks with exploding car bombs and Kalashnikov shots.

'At that time the whole country was full of the same game,' says Bahdoon. For a moment he looks as if he is holding back tears.

'It still is.'

I thought about the thirteen-year-old boy playing war games, on his shoulder an old Russian rifle, in his trembling hand a grenade. The game is real for those whose rifles are sticks and whose grenades are stones, a game for those whose weapons really can kill.

'I was always the leader,' Bahdoon said. 'He wanted to be a prisoner. He sat quietly with his head on his knees and his arms around his legs, and sometimes, when we fed him grasshoppers or made him crawl round the yard, he looked at us as if he'd just woken up from a dream.'

My stomach aches. I see Aslak in the yard in a pale green skirt borrowed from me, fairy wings on his back, looking longingly at the sky as if he might catch a glimpse of the hand of God through the clouds.

'He was so proud,' Bahdoon says. For a moment I imagine that he sees the same picture: little Aslak in a fluttering tulle skirt, his gaze turned towards the darkening sky.

'When he told us he had got into the *istishhad*.'

'Sorry?'

'The suicide brigade. Everyone wants to get into it.'

'Why?'

'What else is there here?' He wipes the corners of his eye rapidly, is silent for a moment before continuing.

'You can be part of a group everyone's afraid of. You can feel you're doing something important. You can go to paradise.'

A gunshot sounds, so close that both Bahdoon and I are startled. The branches of the bushes flutter; the birds take to their wings.

'He asked me to join too. He hated it that I worked for you.'

'Foreigners?'

'Yes. According to him, the only acceptable way of having contact with foreigners was to kill them. I mean . . . you.'

The Kalashnikov rests against Bahdoon's narrow hips as casually as a handbag. He notices what I am looking at and smiles a little, for the first time in the entire conversation.

'Don't be afraid. I don't agree with him.'

'I'm not in the habit of being afraid,' I say. Bahdoon's eyes are gentle and his posture calm; for a moment I want to tell him everything. 'Except for one thing,' I say softly.

'What?'

'Something bad is happening to my brother.'

30

The steps up to my quarters are still warm from the sun. Bahdoon sits as far away from me as I think is possible on the narrow staircase, his cheek against his hand and his long, slim legs crossed. I would like a beer, but for Bahdoon's sake I make us some tea. He never speaks of religion, but I have seen him washing in the corner of the yard, bowing in prayer five times a day. The tea is sweet and pale with milk, crumbs of cinnamon on its surface. When I look for my cigarettes in their hiding place under the steps, Bahdoon, to my surprise, asks if he can have one.

'I didn't know you smoked.'

'I don't.'

'Neither do I.'

The tip of Bahdoon's cigarette glows like a firefly in the darkness; the smoke curling up before his face recalls black-and-white movies and old-fashioned theatres, high ceilings and heavy curtains in front of the screen. In Europe cigarettes are rarely sold at all; here, more than ever. Beside the bomb-ravaged streets rise buildings painted with the logos of tobacco companies; after the bombings they are always the first to be repaired.

I look for news. I try to get hold of Mum, Dad or Aslak. Time passes. The internet is down. This is one of the few places in the world where it is still possible to be isolated for a long time.

Bahdoon's posture is relaxed and his breathing calm. My cheeks are warm and my throat dry. I seek the right words to keep the conversation going, to be interested and polite, not too intrusive, to get Bahdoon to stay and time to pass, to keep him with me until something becomes clear.

'Why did your friend do it?' Wrong question. Hot ash falls onto Bahdoon's thigh. To his eyes I must be incomprehensibly old, unconscionably powerful.

'That is, if you don't mind talking about him?' I continue cautiously, apologetically. I breathe smoke into my lungs, coughing like I did as a twelve-year-old when, with Aslak, I smoked my first and for a long time my last cigarette. In my circle of friends smoking has always been embarrassing, along with getting drunk and casual sex. My school friends were, at fifteen, already like young women, behaving with restraint and dressing in fine clothes, wanting to get married, to have children and to work in business and knowing where to get a stylish rug and the right kind of curtains. For a little while I tried to be like them, to learn the smile deemed appropriate for a woman, the kind that my mother would never learn. When I left, I also wanted to escape from my friends, weekend brunches and the charmingly lit photographs they took of themselves and of me.

'What do you want to know?' Bahdoon asks, draining his glass of tea quickly. Everything I offer is probably luxurious to him.

'Wait a minute,' I say, and go inside. I slice watermelon and mango onto a tray, setting nuts and chocolate brought from Finland down in cups beside the fruit. I turn back and take two bottles of Coca-Cola from the fridge, the old-fashioned, feminine bottles; outside, Bahdoon's eyes are riveted on them as if they were treasure. In the villages the chiefs always offer three drinks: warm Coca-Cola, Sprite and Fanta in narrow glass bottles that you no longer see elsewhere. In some villages the wells have dried up, but there is always lemonade for visitors. I am certain that on the day when life ends on Earth, the last thing left will be a bottle of Coca-Cola, and that the sticky, dark-brown liquid will give rise to new life.

'Everything you want to tell me,' I say, opening the bottles. 'About the two of you. Him. The suicide brigade.'

'Why?' Bahdoon asks, in his voice a metallic tone of doubt. In this country people talk about fear in the same way as Finns discuss the weather. You always have to be looking around you: every empty bottle may explode, anyone can be different from who he says he is, even a small mistake can be fatal. Football and death, news and famine, weddings, hide-and-seek and street bombs belong to the same texture of everyday life whose weight I notice only when I leave, when the plane takes off and lands somewhere where constant caution makes people laugh.

I don't want to scare Bahdoon. It would be dishonest to imagine that we are just chatting here, two equal people. I do not wish to misuse the power that I unavoidably have. I want him to be as comfortable as possible in my presence.

'I know what it's like to love someone who disappears,' I say. I have never said this to anyone else.

He nods.

'He was the best friend I have ever had. Even though he, like you say, disappeared. And did it, that awful thing. I can't talk about him to anyone any more. When I think about him, I always see the face of a child.'

'I have a brother; he disappeared too. I love him. But I don't talk to anyone about him. At school he was a loner. And I avoided him too.' I close my eyes and see the face of the small, shy Aslak. 'Did you know that in some countries they torture people by tying their hands and feet to four different horses and making the horses run in different directions?'

Bahdoon looks at me in astonishment.

'I think they do that here too,' he says.

'I'm sorry. That was a stupid thing to say.'

'Don't worry.'

'I just meant that all of it . . . I felt that I was being torn to shreds. I did everything to be the right sort of person, to fit in with the group. And at the same time there was Aslak, my little brother, who was more important than anyone, and it was him I pushed away.'

I pressed my hands to my face for a moment. The air between my fingers smelled of hibiscus flowers; on the basis of the smell you could have thought you were in paradise.

Bahdoon has not touched his Coca-Cola. He picks up the bottle only when I pass it to him, draining it in one gulp, as if he were afraid I would take it away. When the bottle is empty, I give him the second. He drinks it slowly and appreciatively as if he could find in the drink something new, tastes and nuances typical of this area, this year, whose discernment demands a trained palate.

'I began to make up stories about my brother,' I say quietly. 'I couldn't stand the thought that other people thought he was strange.'

'What kind?' Bahdoon asks, setting the half-empty bottle down on the tray for a moment, but holding on to its neck.

'Stories where he was a hero. I said that he was unusually intelligent, that he coded computer programs and talked about them on the internet with American professors. And that he practised football in secret and could score goals like Zlatan.'

Bahdoon laughed.

'I told the same sorts of stories about myself.'

'You?'

'Yes. I was always hopeless at football. Here all the boys can play.'

'It was the same at our school. It felt as if everyone but my brother was good at it.'

'I prayed for years to have an eye for the ball,' says Bahdoon, smiling. 'Although it didn't even really interest me. I dreamed that I could one day become a researcher, spending my whole life working on one thing.'

I look more closely at Bahdoon. The lamp hanging from the pitched roof of my quarters casts sharp shadows on his face; only now do I notice the wrinkles radiating from the corners of his eyes, still faint like the channel of a river that dried up years ago. He can, after all, not be very many years younger than me; he just looks astonishingly innocent, a boy whom one would want to be able to protect.

'What else did you dream about?'

'That I would be able to leave,' Bahdoon says. 'It is still my greatest dream.' His voice breaks. I bite my lip.

'That was also my greatest dream.' Fortunately I don't say so aloud.

To leave. That was my greatest dream; it still is. I want to go away and stay away. I want to be far away from home. I want to live constantly changing places, like a nomad, to leave as soon as the place begins to feel too familiar, the people too beloved. I want to go forward without looking back, to let my senses fill with the wonder of arriving in a new place, the new smells, the air humidity, the warmth or bone-chilling wind that you encounter when the door of the train or plane opens, when you catch the first glimpse of buildings and step into a city without knowing any of the things that can be found there.

For years I felt as though I were suffocating at home. I was ashamed of my mother, who bought her clothes at flea markets and made vegetarian food that none of my friends wanted to eat. I was angry with my father, who designed parks and swimming places for African children but was never there for school celebrations. I was resentful of Aslak, who was sinking ever deeper into his own world, and at home I could not be what I wanted, an ordinary girl who blended in with the crowd.

In sixth form I realised it was possible to go away. I met a boy who thought my laugh was too noisy and my gaze too deep, whose touch tickled me and did not arouse me at all. I couldn't leave the boy immediately, though, because I was fascinated by his mother. The mother had beautiful clothes and a reticent smile. She worked at a private medical centre, but had travelled the world as a doctor before she was married, vaccinating children in African and Asian villages and living in places where she could only move accompanied by a security guard.

I was fascinated by the photographs she showed me of herself in bone-dry villages, surrounded by goats, sheep and happily grinning children.

Life can also be like that, I thought, and I decided to live with that idea. *It is possible to go away and begin your own life somewhere where no one knows you.* I stopped drinking, took up running and yoga, excelled in my matriculation exams and started studying medicine the following autumn.

I got away. I can always leave when I want to. I travel to countries where everyone wants to get away, but few of those who leave get to their destination. I am either working or a tourist, wearing a collared shirt and a helmet, or I travel with a rucksack on my back wearing the kind of floaty skirt tourists buy in the local markets. I am often despondent or unhappy, but I am only seldom in danger and even then I am surrounded by an entire system that will ensure my safety. If I am ill,

I can go home. If the country is threatened by natural disaster or conflict, I can go home. I have insurance that ensures that a helicopter will take me to a well-equipped hospital from anywhere in the world; my passport will allow me to cross all borders, back and forth; I have a savings account and a home which I can leave without checking the surroundings and to which it is always possible to return.

I close my eyes. Into my mind slip images of young people, little girls trapped in the quietness of small towns and boys who dance in front of the mirror, and the girls and boys of entirely different small towns, dark hair and eyes like coals, children wearing clothes collected from Western recycling projects, how they all dream of leaving, how all those dreams could rise simultaneously into the air, making the wind that blows across borders thick and heavy.

'Tell me more about your brother,' Bahdoon says. I narrow my eyes, even though it is dark, rubbing my left palm with the thumb of my right hand, and return to a real, completely dreamlike moment.

'When we were little, we almost always slept side by side. If one of us woke up with a nightmare or to the sound of Mum and Dad arguing, we squeezed each other by the hand. I thought we would always be together.'

The crickets chirp around us. The sky is cloudless and the constellation of the Pleiades bright.

'My father and my grandfather looked at the stars to determine the beginning of the growing season,' says Bahdoon.

'And then there weren't any proper growing seasons any longer,' I say, and he looks me in the eye, the outlines of my own face reflected in his eyes.

'Yes. Why are you afraid something is happening to your brother?'

Bahdoon has drained the second bottle too. Slices of mango in the shape of fishing boats stand in a row on the tray; in the ripe flesh the fibres are clearly visible. I think of the velvet-sweet fruit between my teeth. I cannot imagine when I will next be able to eat.

'At this moment in Finland someone is shooting people from a rooftop.'

'Has he killed many people?'

'I don't know. The internet isn't working.'

'You're afraid your brother is there?'

'I'm afraid he's the gunman.'

'Your brother?'

'Whenever something like this happens, the first person I think of is him.'

'Why?'

'There's something about him ... there's been something like that about him for a long time. As if he's shut himself off completely from other people. We text sometimes. And then, in some texts, he's said things that frighten me.'

Bahdoon takes a slice of mango and sucks the flesh from the skin. I offer the tray to encourage him to take more. I hope he will feel he can eat his fill and go when he wants to.

'My best friend said everything straight out,' Bahdoon says. 'He waited for years to get into the suicide brigade. It was his dream. He thought it was the purest thing possible. To kill people for a good cause.'

Something touches my neck. I wave my hand. A large, flying cockroach flies off. It has transparent wings and a body covered by a hard shell that drips with slime when you hit it.

'It is pure to kill people for a good cause. My brother wrote in the same way. Pure.'

'What was the cause?'

'What?'

'The good cause. The thing you could kill for.'

I look for one of Aslak's messages. I read it aloud to Bahdoon, translating the most important parts into Somali.

'I am drowning in this shit. Everything is polluted. The whole of Western culture is just one hedonistic performance. The civilisation we're so proud of died a long time ago. Our only religion is the belief that we have the right to everything we want. The only human right is the human's right to consume. That right destroys everything.'

Bahdoon makes a flower out of the mango skin. The murmur of French voices from the other side of the yard grows gradually louder. I can make out Gerard's voice, the slightly overenthusiastic, tinkling laugh he uses in big groups. Bahdoon takes a piece of chocolate from the tray, breaks it in half and eats. He is silent for such a long time that I smooth my skirt and rise. My thigh muscles have gone numb and the wind is too cool. I begin to clear the dishes, avoiding making too much sound.

'My friend talked about the same thing,' Bahdoon says quietly. 'That Western culture is all of that. Hedonism. Sick consumption. Polluted.'

'And in his opinion it was pure to try to destroy everything associated with it?

'That's what he said. But I don't believe that was really the issue.'

'What, then?'

'The fact that he wanted to escape.'

'Like all of us,' I said, so quietly that Bahdoon doesn't necessarily hear me. More loudly, I say: 'Thank you for the company.'

'Likewise,' Bahdoon answers. 'And for the food.'

Bahdoon disappears behind the high sage bushes. The internet is working again. I set the tray back down on the step and search for the Finnish news.

31

'Nothing irrevocable has happened yet.'
He stops shooting. For a moment. To get time to think. It already seems like a mistake. His thoughts press so hard that his head feels heavy. The lightness he felt a moment ago is gone; his limbs are heavy and stiff, hard to move.

This may end badly, he thinks, feeling the fine spider feet of panic beneath his skin. The police have cordoned off the area. He has been surrounded; inside the ring, besides the police, there are only people lying on the ground, wounded or dead; he is not sure whether he has killed any of them.

The police have delivered an old-fashioned phone to him using a drone. The drone is almost the same as the toy he used to play with as a child with his big sister and his father. It rose quietly buzzing through the air; blue lights flashed on the rotor blades. For a moment he was a little boy again, enchanted by the silver-sided toy that was coming towards him.

He has read about this kind of situation. He has wolfed down thrillers and news reports, the internet's mass-murder websites' detailed explanations of how the police act in this kind of situation, what kind of psychological method they use in their conversations with the gunman, how snipers try to ensure that nothing fateful will happen. He imagines the policeman who will talk to him sitting in a van surrounded by a negotiating group, with the officer directing the situation stationed opposite in a parked car.

'Nothing irrevocable has happened yet.' It is the right sort of phrase, calming and hopeful with regard to the situation; the intention is to get him to participate in a dialogue, to show that the police are on his side, to show that it is possible for him to surrender with honour.

He squeezes the phone in his hands. His breathing is heavy; words will not come. The city is quiet. The thick fog that has persisted for some days hides the empty streets and buildings; only the blue lights of the police cars and ambulances glow through it. The streets have been closed and the trams and cars directed to more distant roads; the restaurants, shops, hotels, cinemas and railway station emptied. Only in the restaurant on the top floor of the department store is there movement. He imagines how somewhere in that restaurant, behind the tinted windows, a police marksman is standing, taking aim at him.

On the asphalt lie four people, each of whom he has shot. A woman his mother's age and another, much older. A man in a fancy suit and a woman whose breast the man was caressing as they walked. Not one bullet to the head, although that is where he was aiming. Shoulder, side, stomach, leg.

He wanted to join the army, but was not accepted; he was not the kind of material that was needed to protect the country. The wounded people are still alive, or so he believes. His aim was not accurate enough; it seems like a humiliation. This was supposed to be done cleanly and quickly, but the wounded are a job half done, a mess he can't clean up, a trail that reveals everything about him.

He also aimed at a young mother, holding the hand of a small child who was walking uncertainly. He did not press the trigger. He could not go on.

He sees massive vehicles driving along the empty street. They look strange, as if from another world. Perhaps nothing that is happening is real after all. The army tanks approach him.

Is this the beginning of war? he thinks, and the thought is a flame, hot and mesmerising.

Are they all at war against me?

32

The tanks roll forward to protect the doctors, the nurses and the police. He cannot do anything. He is powerless, surrounded, humiliated.

The ambulance drives through the police cordon. The people he has shot are lifted onto stretchers. Siren howling, the ambulance drives through the deserted city. He wonders why the driver is sounding the siren even though the streets are empty. He hopes the people will survive. He hopes they will die. He hopes he himself will die soon, or just disappear.

His head hurts. Everything is foggy and confused; he would like to jump head first off the roof, to fall to the asphalt and for everything to be over.

He eases the weapon into his hand. He feels the marksman's gaze, the hands lifting the weapon, the soldiers in the tanks, the police, everyone, become alert around him. They are waiting to see what he will do next. He has no idea what to do. The butt of the rifle is smooth and cool against his hand. The city is beautiful in a new way, the police cars' lights glowing as if someone has put them there to create atmosphere. His clothes are wet and his heavy breathing hurts his chest. He is cold and he is hungry.

As children, when Dad and Mum argued, he and his sister made a den under the covers and he climbed into his sister's lap. They had a torch and his sister read him a story; he felt the warmth of his sister's breath on his neck and thought he could spend his whole life like this, in a dark burrow under the soft, sweet-smelling covers.

He wants to go under those covers now. Into a small space where the air is warm from breathing, with no room for anyone but him and his sister. His sister's strong hand would smooth the nightmares away.

He wants to take everything back and walk back along the days, the weeks, the months and the years, to return to a time when everything was just beginning and no one expected anything from him. He wants his sister to have a soft nightdress and a book that they both love. He wants to be small and curl up in his sister's arms.

33

'We can't afford to give up hope.'

That is what his mother said in the lectures she gave for students, those incomprehensibly optimistic-looking young people. Years ago he often went and listened to his mother's lectures. The things his mother talked about allowed him to forget for a moment the alienation he felt among people.

When he listened to his mother and watched the students enthusiastically taking notes on their computers, it felt as if someone had pulled back a camera from a close-up to take in the whole world. Nowhere, nowhere at all, was he an issue. It was a perfectly liberating thought. The issue was something bigger, something much more important than what he felt.

The world may be headed for destruction, he thought, his mind full of horror and burning zeal. How many possibilities it opened up, how much more merciful it was. A whole world does not need any one person on its side; everyone is needed to save it from destruction.

Me too, he thought then. *It is possible that this world needs me too.*

In addition to his mother's lectures, he began to read other things. He read long reports which described what would become of the world if climate change continued. He read about businesses that prospected for more oil in the most fragile corners of the globe, even though they already had enough fossil fuels to destroy the entire world. He read about deserted villages and cities ravaged by floods, people who left their homes and never found a place to sleep in peace. He read about felled rainforests and coral reefs that were in danger of disappearing completely. He read about the Great Pacific garbage patch, which may be twice the size of the United States.

In reading, he forgot himself. All his attention was directed at the environment: nature, which was wild and stupefyingly functional, and at the same time fragile and in danger of destruction. He thought of the tortoises floating in oceans that had existed long before people, their steady swimming and their slowly turning heads. The fact that human activity threatened the existence of such creatures made him feel pure hatred towards the whole of humanity.

All of this brought him closer to his mother. He was there when his mother returned home after speaking to members of parliament about how important it was to limit fossil fuel emissions with stricter legislation. His mother's mouth was pursed tight and there was a broken blood vessel in her eye; she put her coat and shoes away with the tenseness of a leopard preparing to leap, poured herself a glass of wine and said to his father: 'I felt like throwing the whole lot of them out of the room. Grown-up people. Our decision makers. The elite of society. Sitting there and pissing around with each other while I tried to explain how they could save the world as even a semi-tolerable place for their own children. Clowns! Asking stupid questions and harping on about so-called facts, every one of which is wrong. Praising the achievements of their own party and complaining about the faults of others as if there were an election coming!'

He listened intently as his mother expressed her anger against the minister who wanted to send Finnish icebreakers to the Arctic to look for oil.

'Every literate person knows that if we want to preserve the world as at least somehow habitable for future generations, we have to stop states and businesses from using the greater part of the fossil fuels they already have. And these . . . these slimy, immoral, lizard-brained morons want to send government equipment to drill for oil in an area where it is catastrophic for the environment.' Mum dropped her wine glass on the floor and bent down to pick up the shards with her bare hands. Her collarbone rose under the neck of her blouse as sharp as if someone had gnawed away the flesh around it; the hand that was gathering the glass trembled.

'Sometimes I hope that the Black Death will come back and wipe us all out.'

He absorbed it all into himself, the frustrated rage that could have been his own. Dad went on reading from his tablet as if Mum were talking about some everyday incident. When the sinews in Mum's neck tautened, he felt the tightness in his own limbs too, and when Mum walked up to Dad and tore the tablet away from him, he too wanted to tear something.

'I'm talking to you!' Mum shouted at Dad, brushing the pieces of glass from the floor into a dustpan and gesturing for him to stay away.

'And I'm listening,' Dad said, clenching his hands into fists.

'How hard is it to ignore that screen for an instant?'

'There's no alternative any more, thanks very much.'

'Why don't you just piss off, then?'

'Really. You've been at home for three minutes and you're already suggesting we split up.'

'I wasn't talking about splitting up.'

And so they went on. Dad and Mum, who before the birth of himself and his big sister travelled around the world studying devastated places that could be made beautiful.

He withdrew into his room, went online and found people who read the same texts as he did, who felt the same passionate frustration. When he heard the argumentative voices of Mum and Dad on the other side of the door, he was on Mum's side. He was always on Mum's side. Mum was beautiful and brave, even if Dad could never see it.

He was also at Mum's side when she had to go on a nature hike for a couple of days to sort out her thoughts.

He walked behind his mother through a forest where there was nothing to be heard but the beating of birds' wings startled into flight and the soughing of pine branches. After the dense greenness the boulders continued as wide open as the sea and in the morning as they left the tent they could see a fox slipping behind the trees. He smelled the scent of damp trees warmed by the sun, sat on the boulders in the darkness of a cloudy evening. Here, the darkness seemed denser than in the city, an all-enveloping blackness in whose recesses anything at all might be creeping, but which did not seem threatening, but liberating, a resting place in which he, too, could curl up and hide.

They walked in single file with their rucksacks, their tents and their sleeping bags on their backs, talking about birds, trees and plants, and were quiet, boiling water on a campfire and mixing with it, in the morning, porridge flakes, at lunch soup powder, for supper pasta, in the afternoon instant coffee and sugar, with chocolate, raisins and nuts. His muscles hurt. His shoes were too hard and when he was walking downhill they pressed on his toes until a dark, bloody sludge gathered under his big toenails. He enjoyed the pain. He enjoyed the feeling that all of his body was in use, every muscle had its job, had a path to follow, and everything was clear and simple. When they stopped to eat, he was so hungry that the food made from packets of powder seemed a wonderful pleasure. And when they put up their tent and spread their sleeping bags on the ground, he was so tired that he fell asleep as soon as he had zipped up his sleeping bag.

If only I could live like this, he thought then.

If only I could just walk onwards, smell the scent of bark, twigs and fallen leaves and listen to sounds, not one of which is caused by human beings.

When they returned home, Mum and Dad decided to go to a yoga camp together. He felt stronger than ever, firm and connected to the ground. He decided to seek out people who experienced the power of nature in the same way as he did, who breathed more freely in the dark forest, who felt the same overwhelming rage about how people were flaying the world of all that was pure and beautiful.

As he stepped into the high-ceilinged main room of the old wood cabin, he immediately knew he had made a mistake. 'Welcome Evening for New Members' had been the message on the environmental organisation's website. He abhorred people and avoided new situations. Nevertheless he had signed up for the evening. It must be Mum's fault. Mum's, and that stupid hike's, his bloody toes and the deer that ran across the path with its fawn as if giving a sign. Animals running into the coppice, owls looking on from the branches of the spruces, the stream whose water could be drunk from your cupped hands, the darkness that hid mind and body – all this had fooled him.

He had imagined that somewhere there would be people bound together by that experience: a group of young people, at home in the shadows, for whom words were difficult and silence a relief, who feared people as much as they yearned for them and for whom darkness was a place of safety in a world which wanted to shine light on even the most sensitive matters. He had wanted to believe that somewhere there might be a tribe he could join, an army of soldiers with dark eyes and bad postures would come together to fight for something more beautiful than the culture created by humankind, for something eternal and holy.

When he saw the people gathered round the long table, he wanted to run away. Sweat formed into droplets on his temples and his breath wheezed; a stench rose from his armpits and his hair, despite its morning wash, stuck to his forehead in greasy lumps. He took a step backwards and almost stumbled on the threshold, grabbing the doorpost for support. At that moment a vigorous, cool, sweatless hand grasped his. A fine-featured man, perhaps a couple of years older than he was, who looked as if everything was effortless for him, as if he ran to work and cycled all year round, as if he was able to smile genially and always find the right words in conversation, pulled him up with a strong grip.

'Welcome!' the man said, guiding him to a free chair among other equally energetic, equally clean, equally intolerably dynamic-looking people. He felt the beating of his heart and the heat of his cheeks, wiped his sweaty palm on his jeans, which had looked good in the shop but looked awful on. 'Hi!' he said to the girl sitting beside him, who had long, blond hair and wore no make-up. In her perfectly fitting jeans and simple sweater, the girl looked so natural and self-confident that she could just as well be attending a presidential dinner. On his other side sat a dark-haired girl in a close-fitting checked shirt, her voice husky and her speech rapid and opposite them effortlessly elegant girls and boys who talked as if they had always known each other. On their cheeks was the glow of outdoor life and exuberance, and their muscles were so toned that you could imagine them climbing the sheerest cliffs, happy smiles on their faces.

No one responded to his greeting. He summoned his courage and muttered again: 'Hi.' His voice rose, ringing out loudly in the midst of the group, which had suddenly fallen silent, and making everyone around the table turn to stare at him.

'Well, hi!' said the man who had helped him up, and suddenly everyone began to laugh, everyone but him. He pressed his nails into the palms of his hands and smiled, with such determination that he must have looked like a halfwit; he smiled half-wittedly all evening while a young man spoke passionately about the state of the environment, the work of the organisation and the importance of *inspiring others.*

'We must be the change that we wish to see in the world,' the man said, and everyone around him began to clap.

He hung his head and looked at his thighs in their badly fitting jeans, and the palms which rested on them, bloated by medicines and damp with sweat. There was nothing in him which anyone, least of all himself, would want to see in the world.

34

Laura

'I love them.' I am not sure whether I say this to the police or to myself. I am not sure whether I say it at all or just imagine it, but the words are somewhere, and after them rise more words, a deluge of words. I love my children more than anything else. I was not always a good mother. I'm not sure if I was ever a good mother. Is it possible to be sometimes good, sometimes bad? If you are bad enough, does it invalidate all the good?

My words break. I break. The policeman brings me a glass of water and the woman squeezes my hand. Her hand is warm and dry; unpolished nails, on the back of her left hand a liver spot, on her fourth finger a white gold ring.

The woman is my age or a little younger. Her shift must end sometime. After this evening, her life will go on as before; she will be able to keep her friends and her dreams and her interests, decide whether to spend Christmas abroad or to invite the children for dinner at home. She will be able to go to concerts and the theatre, to retire and say she is having the time of her life.

'Four people are wounded,' she says.

'They have been taken to hospital. They are in a critical condition. The situation is calm at the moment.' I nod as I nodded at school when the teacher talked about Aslak, lowering her voice; I nod in the way that I nodded at the health centre and at the child psychiatrist's. I am ready to accept everything that is to come.

'We hope that you can give us information about your son that will help us resolve the situation,' the policewoman says.

For a moment I am sure they are mistaken. My son can have nothing to do with what is happening now. *My son is a little child. My son is a child*, I think, and an iron fist squeezes my heart and my lungs into a bony ball. *My son is a child!*

My son sits in his stroller, a toy aeroplane in his hand, smiling at everything he sees. He has soft wrists and dimples in his knees and he often sits quietly for a long time, his eyebrows wrinkled and his lower lip pushed out. He likes trains, tractors and princess dresses, and wants, when we read him stories, to check who's a goody and who's a baddy. He can sing in tune, but doesn't score goals at football; when he listens to music he starts to dance. When he grows up, he wants to be a guitarist and an astronaut. He goes to church with his nursery and one evening announces that he believes in God. He always wants to play with his big sister and she only lets him sometimes; but then sometimes he doesn't want to play even when his big sister asks him to. He smiles at everyone and everyone loves him for that reason. He can put his toes in his mouth and make his lips splutter. For his third birthday he chooses sweets and he learns to say his Ss at the shop till. He calls me from the shopping centre loo on Eerik's phone and says:

'Thweets, thweets, Mum, I can say eth!' and I laugh and ask him to say it again, 'eat thweets only thometimes, thing thome thilly thongs, thix thox thit in a think.'

My son is a child. He smiles at everyone who looks at him. He won't hurt anyone and no one is allowed to hurt him.

The policeman starts the tape recorder.

'Are you ready?'

'I am,' I reply. I am not.

'A young man is on the roof of the Glass Palace with a gun. He has shot four people, who are seriously injured. On the basis of a message left on the internet the police suspect that the gunman is your son, Lauri Aslak Anttila.'

I nod. I am a fly on the roof, tiny, a creature that eats rubbish and excrement, which can be killed with one well-aimed blow.

'Did you have knowledge of your son's plans?'

I shake my head. I nod.

'No. Or yes. It depends how you look at it.'

'Can you be more specific?'

'He has . . . Aslak has had thoughts which . . . because of which it is not a complete surprise that . . .'

'What sort of thoughts?'

I press my hands to my face.

'I never believed that he would really . . .'

'Are you able to continue?'

'I am.'

'What kind of thoughts?'

'About mass murder.'

'Yes?'

'I remember a conversation, many years ago. At the dinner table. At lunch, or was it dinner. I think we had Indian food.'

'Yes?'

'It was after some school murder. We read the news and he . . . he said that it couldn't simply be condemned.'

'What couldn't?'

'Killing classmates. That if . . . He said that physical violence should not be the only thing to be condemned. That . . . violence always happens in relation to something else. That it can also be seen as a reaction to another kind of violence. For example, if a person is treated as if he is invisible.'

'Did he speak often about the same subject?'

'It developed into an argument between him and my husband. But somehow . . . when he read news of such deeds, he was always . . . it seemed as if he was fascinated by them.'

'Did he have any kind of psychiatric diagnosis?'

'In secondary school he was diagnosed with severe depression.'

'Did he go to therapy?'

'He was prescribed medicines. But he only took them for a short while. He tried therapy, but . . . he didn't like his first therapist. We couldn't find anyone he would agree to see.'

The room around me changes. Aslak is sitting opposite me, his head in his hands. A teenage Aslak with bad posture, who sits with his head in his hands and doesn't notice that I am looking at him.

'We tried to find help for you,' I say to Aslak. I do not cry.

'I'm sorry?'

'I meant for him. We tried to find help for him. But it . . . we never really knew what it should be. It felt as if we were completely alone with him.'

The policewoman gives me a glass of water. When Aava whinged as a child, I also gave her water. When

I was tired and did not know what else to do, I poured a glass of cold water and made her drink it. Aslak almost never whinged. I never needed to calm him.

'Who else knew about these thoughts of his?'

'Myself and my husband. And my daughter, I'm sure. But the thoughts weren't clear. You must understand that. He never came home and said he intended to kill someone. He . . . he is the world's sweetest boy.'

'Did he talk about these matters later, as an adult?'

'No. Or sometimes. At the beginning of university.'

'He is still registered at Helsinki University?'

'Yes. In the philosophy faculty. With a minor in environmental science. He got in with top marks. But he didn't . . . he didn't really feel at home there.'

'And at the beginning, at university, he . . .?'

'For a moment he had a group of friends. I was extraordinarily happy at the beginning. They were smart, well-behaved, well-dressed young people. But there was something . . . at some point it . . . in what he said there began to be . . .'

'What?'

'It was a good time. I want to stress that. The beginning was great, a good time. Eerik and I thought, at last, he is finding his own place, his own group of friends. At that time we met up very seldom, but when we did meet . . . he was apt to make extraordinarily negative comments about people.'

'Who, for example?'

'Homeless people. Alcoholics. The unemployed. Anyone who couldn't cope with life. There was something chilling about it. Many people think like that, of course. But all the values we had tried to teach at home . . .'

'What did he say?'

'He called them subhuman. Weaker elements. And sometimes he said . . . they should be got rid of.'

'Was he still in contact with his friends?'

'No. As far as I know. I think not. The next thing that happened was that . . . he was suspended.'

The policewoman nods.

'Did you know anything about it?'

'The police went through his flat and his computer.'

'My grandmother's flat?'

'The one he lives in.'

My grandfather never came back from the war. My grandmother brought my mother up alone, working at the factory and as a maid to a rich but lonely gentleman in a large country house. During the day my grandmother cooked fishcakes and herring in tomato sauce for the gentleman; at night she listened to the gentleman drowsily swilling cognac telling stories about how there was no one around him who really understood him, no one to laugh at his jokes or notice when he was sad. When the gentleman began to nod in the old armchair in my grandmother's room, she put the nightcap back on his head, led him to his bed and had time for a couple of hours' sleep before it was time to wake up to knead the morning's bread. My grandmother had a quiet voice and hard hands whose strength she used when my mother was in the way, or when she complained that she was afraid in her room at night when my grandmother was listening to the gentleman's endless tale of loneliness.

My mother did her homework in the little servant's room in the big house, watching as visiting children, the gentleman's relatives, set the table with rose-patterned porcelain crockery in the pale-blue Wendy house whose door she was not allowed to open, and dreaming that one day she would find the Wendy house's keys and would, while the others slept, creep in to make the dolls tea out of rainwater and cake out of daisies.

Granny set aside a little from every pay packet in order to have something that no one could take from her. After she retired, she bought a flat, one room plus a kitchen alcove; she dabbed rouge on her cheeks and her lips, put a green felt hat on her head and a flowered scarf round her neck and took me to Fazer's café to eat ice cream.

'A woman needs a door so that she can lock everyone else out,' she said to me, before her a delicate coffee cup and a pastry covered in green marzipan, and

I thought about the cupboard where I had hidden raisins and nuts against the days when my mother's eyes turned into cold, gleaming coins. I never told Granny about those days, even when she squeezed my hand as gently as she could with her bony bird-fingers and said: 'Remember, won't you, that you can tell me everything?'

But I knew I couldn't tell her about my mother. I knew that it was my job to protect her, to keep secret the moments that were too ugly for anyone else's eyes, to hide the image of my mother that only I could see.

That flat, the little room and kitchen alcove for which Granny saved all her life and of which she was, right up to her death, enormously proud, was now being searched by the police. They were searching Aslak's computer and phone for images, messages and websites he had visited, everything he had written or read, everything he had left behind him. Every morning Granny had dusted the bookshelves, displaying the porcelain cats and dogs she had collected, and the glass ball in which snow fell on two skating girls when you shook it. She would stand, wearing her apron, in the kitchen alcove, cooking French toast and listening to a talk programme on the radio. She would open the window and whisper to me: 'Listen. A nightingale.'

What would she have said if she had known what was happening in her flat now?

PART
FOUR

However, no country will be immune to the violent consequences of global climate change.

CRAIG A. ANDERSON and MATT DELISI
'Implications of Global Climate Change for Violence in Developed and Developing Countries', 'Implications of Global Climate Change for Violence'
(Iowa State University)

35

Human filth. Secret group.

Übermensch:
What's this all about?
AryanKing:
It's not about anything.
Übermensch:
Why didn't you come yesterday?
StateIsMyBitch:
We did. We went to a different place.
Übermensch:
What am I not getting?
AryanKing:
We wanted to go on without you.
Übermensch:
What?
StateIsMyBitch:
You know.
Übermensch:
I don't.

AryanKing:
We can't afford to keep your sort with us.
Übermensch:
What sort?
StateIsMyBitch:
Losers.
AryanKing:
Psychos.
Übermensch:
Is this a joke?
StateIsMyBitch:
Don't play dumb.
Übermensch:
What?
AryanKing:
WHATWHATWHAT? The pills. The loony bin. Half
  a year off university.
Übermensch:
Who told you?
StateIsMyBitch:
Well, it certainly wasn't you. If it was, we might even
  respect you.
AryanKing:
Maybe.
Übermensch:
That was a long time ago.
StateIsMyBitch:
Why didn't you tell us?

Übermensch:
It never occurred to me. I didn't think it mattered.
AryanKing:
No? 'What would society really lose if the weaker
  elements were allowed to fade away naturally?'
  A direct quote from you.
Übermensch:
So what?
StateIsMyBitch:
You're the weaker element.

36

Beautiful death. Secret group.

Someoneisoutthere:
Why did you change your name?
Earthsong:
I realised it was stupid.
Someoneisoutthere:
It was about time.
Earthsong:
Oh, you think so too?
Someoneisoutthere:
Absolutely.
Earthsong:
Why didn't you say?
Someoneisoutthere:
I knew you would realise it for yourself.
Earthsong:
Nice that there's someone who has faith in my
   intelligence.

Someoneisoutthere:
Absolutely. Your intelligence and your heart.
Earthsong:
Are things going better?
Someoneisoutthere:
A black eye.
Earthsong:
Again?
Someoneisoutthere:
It won't end until I die.
Earthsong:
You've got to object!
Someoneisoutthere:
I daren't.
Earthsong:
You've got to. It will kill you otherwise. Don't give it
    that satisfaction.

37

Someoneisoutthere:
I left today.
Earthsong:
For good?
Someoneisoutthere:
For good.
Earthsong:
Where are you?
Someoneisoutthere:
Safe.
Earthsong:
Definitely?
Someoneisoutthere:
Definitely.
Earthsong:
Fantastic! My brave girl!
Someoneisoutthere:
Say it again.
Earthsong:
What?

Someoneisoutthere:
MY girl.
Earthsong:
MY girl.
Someoneisoutthere:
Thank you.

38

Earthsong. That is the name which his friends called him. Before that he was Übermensch, but that was a stupid, ridiculous and childish phase. At that time his thinking was immature, still forming and everything about him fragile and easily fooled. He scorns the self of that period; scorns his friends who claimed to be his friends but weren't, who read Ayn Rand and parroted Nietzsche's thoughts without understanding anything about them and believed themselves to be special, those whom nature had selected to win.

His new friends live in London, Buenos Aires, New York, Cape Town and Delhi, and he has not met any of them. His friends have names like *Sturmunddrang*, *Killthemall* and *Elmundo*. In their pictures they look like he does in his: pale and dark eyed in their black clothes; the photographs are so skilfully lit and edited that only carefully highlighted parts of their faces are visible. He likes photographs like that. They show enough, but not too much; the face is left to the viewer's imagination and that is exactly what he has always wanted, that the environment and people should be under the cover of darkness, that everything should not be so unprotected and on show, that people should close their mouths, hide their faces and keep their feelings and their thoughts to themselves.

This society of pseudonymous, unknown friends in their dramatically lit photographs is the first group to which he has felt he belongs, the first cohort of people with whom, in conversation, he has been able to forget himself, his complete outsiderdom, and concentrate on exchanging ideas.

He converses with them from the small flat on whose hall floor his granny was found dead. The flat's windows have been closed for so long that when you come in you are met by the stink of sweat, beer and banana skins that are growing green fuzz. But the only people who come in from outside are the pizza delivery man and the shop delivery man; Mum tries sometimes, but he always finds a reason to stop her, and he himself goes out as seldom as possible. The flat is his nest; he tries to make it as cosy and warm as the covers he and his sister curled up under as children.

He has talked to his friends a bit about music, books and movies, and very little about family, friends or girl- or boyfriends. They have talked a lot about the environment and violence. They have shared pictures of cities inundated by floods, destroyed mining areas, earth cracked with drought. He has searched for romantic pictures of forests, a tree flowering in the middle of a polluted city, a chameleon on a bush branch. They have written about Osama bin Laden, Ulrike Meinhof and young men dressed in long black coats who shot persons known and unknown in schools, universities or on the street. Some of them admire those men, some despise them.

'Violence must have some greater aim. Shooting people just because you're pissed off or want revenge is just as pathetic as being obsessed by clothes made in sweatshops or showing off with an expensive handbag.'

That is what he wrote after a young Finnish man stole a rifle from the army and traipsed through the forest to a class reunion to shoot his former classmates.

That was when Saharaflower appeared on his screen for the first time.

'I agree,' wrote the girl, whom he had never talked to before.

'Violence is acceptable as a political tool, not as an instrument for one's own therapy or to prop up a broken ego.'

Saharaflower's picture was different from the others'. It was taken in natural light in Libya, at the gate of the medieval town of Ghadames. Her eyes, which were looking straight at the camera, looked open and brave, ready to take on anyone and everyone. Sahara-flower had pale skin and dark eyes and her face was framed by a silver, glimmering scarf; on her head were sunglasses decorated with diamonds. The girl's cheekbones were high and a smile rippled across her full lips. The girl looked as if she belonged in an advertisement or one of the countless music videos in which women in headscarves perform fast-paced songs about hatred.

He responded quickly.

'Good that there's someone who understands. I'm perturbed by people who love violence for its own sake. Or who think it is the ultimate way of getting attention.'

'Same here. Here too there are far too many guys who think that killing someone is a good way of putting a plaster on their own egos.'

'I'll kill others so that I will finally be noticed.'

'Those clowns use the number of their victims to compete.'

'Exactly. Never mind about the content, as long as you kill more people than someone else.'

'As long as I can get the world's attention for myself for a moment.'

'Pathetic.'

'They think they're doing something amazing. Revolutionary. Really it's just this narcissistic, attention-seeking culture, spreading its pictures everywhere and measuring its own well-being with millions of different yardsticks, taken to its extreme.'

'I'll kill them all, because I'm worth it.'

When they had finished their conversation, his face felt odd. Unknowingly, he had begun to smile.

On the day when the voyage to the North Pole began, he wrote to his friend, his fingers trembling.

'For 130,000 years nothing like this has happened. Massive. Who is following this?'

'The Greenpeace ship is going.'

'Hippies are staging performances at the harbour.'

'PERFORMANCES?! No fucking way.'

'Hippies will save the world by painting themselves green and standing on their heads.'

'How long do they intend to go on?'

'A couple of generations more?'

'The blood will go to their heads.'

'That will make a good cocktail, mixed with piss.'

'This really is crushing.'

'What do you mean?'

'When I was a child, my mother told me that the melting of the ice so you could sail to the North Pole would be the last straw. That it would make human-kind realise that we don't have time to think about what to do: we have to act. That then, at the very latest, everyone would have to understand that if we go on as before, civilisation will be destroyed.'

'And now it's happening.'

Saharaflower had joined the conversation.

He looked at the girl smiling on the screen for a long time. As he breathed it felt as if someone were blowing up a balloon inside him. Warmth rose to his cheeks and he wrote his response quickly and calmly.

'It is happening. And nothing is changing. The decision makers are talking about the same things as twenty years ago. And most people believe that all consumption means is calories, and emissions are their own farts.'

'I won't even say what I'd like to do to the guys who imagine they are promoting some political goal with *performances!*'

'I can imagine what you're not saying. It's exactly that attitude that makes our generation mere losers. People think that *performance* and *action* are the same thing. That the fact that I *pay attention* to something (i.e. I have an opinion about something) can really have an effect.'

'I think those guys don't even imagine that. Most people our age don't even think about action, only performance. There is just the *self* performing some opinion or emotion.'

He wrote it with his heart pounding, his limbs burning with the thought that on the other side of the world there was a wide-eyed girl who was interested in what he had to say.

'Exactly. At one time people took photographs to communicate something about the world to others, some fleeting observation or moment. Our parents' generation turned the camera on themselves, and now a photograph means a picture of *me* doing something.'

'It's the same now with violent attacks. Instead of being a means of attaining a goal, there's just *me me me* being violent.'

'It's exactly that that makes the school killers despicable. Violence is the strongest political resource. It is unforgivably pathetic to use it because *I* want revenge because *I* have been treated wrongly.'

'Real terrorists have something bigger than themselves. Religion or an ideal on account of which they kill.'

'What do you think of it as a means?'

'Terrorism?'

'Violence.'

'Historically it hasn't been very successful.'

'Depends on your point of view. For example the Nazis succeeded, at the beginning, very well in their own terms. North Korea has succeeded from the point of view of its leaders for a phenomenally long time. ISIS succeeded revolutionarily well. And if you think about us, too, Gaddafi's government stayed in power precisely because of its all-pervasive, tightly controlled machine of violence. From his point of view it, too, was highly successful.'

Something in the girl's words was at the same time frightening and fascinating. He could almost feel her slim fingers around his arm, pulling him towards some new, unknown path.

'I don't completely agree with their aims.'

'But that wasn't the point.'

'What was?'

'The fact that the success of violence depends on your viewpoint. Think of the world as a whole. Power rests with those who have the strongest and most effective machinery of violence. I'd be prepared to bet that from the point of view of the USA, for example, violence, or at least the control of an effective machinery of violence, has achieved a great deal.'

They exchanged messages all night long about the melting of the ice caps and the nature of political violence. In the early hours they told each other jokes which were not particularly good, but whose cleverness each of them praised because they wanted to please the other. And they talked about what the stars look like above the desert surrounding Ghadames, what it is like to climb the dunes and slide down them and how it feels to stay awake on the shore of a Finnish lake until the rising sun bleaches the summer night into morning and mist moves on the surface of the lake. When they finally finished the conversation to go to sleep, it was already morning. Sunlight penetrated into his room despite the blackout curtains he had so carefully closed. Generally the light hurt his eyes, but now he slept a deep sleep until the afternoon and, when he woke, he opened the windows as he had not done in a long time, took a shower and went out.

That day he walked around the city as if in a foreign country, strolling in the parks and along the shore and stopping to feed the mallards and to look at people, drink coffee from paper cups and buy ice cream from the kiosk he had visited as a child with his father, his mother and his sister the first time he had been able to ride a bike without stabilisers. With the spring wind on his face he thought about riding fast and far away, leaving his family behind and zooming on his little bike towards unknown countries. It was comforting that the kiosk was still in the same place, the same metal chairs under the canopy as when he was little, at the back of the kiosk a shelf of liquorice sweets.

He walked around the city until sunset, imagining himself to be an alien from outer space, one for whom the human body was borrowed and who followed the sad, happy, dreaming and absent-looking people around him with an outsider's interest, without any idea of the nature of the fear and grief of human life.

When he returned home in the evening, Saharaflower was already waiting for him. Generally he conversed with his new friends in open chats, but now Saharaflower had sent him a private message.

'It was nice to chat yesterday,' she said.

'Yes, it was,' he replied.

'I felt you understand a bit better than the others.'

'Same here.'

The tips of his fingers were sweating. Even though Saharaflower was only a picture on a screen, he felt that he had never got so close to a girl. His only experiences of girls were frosty humiliations. After them he had hated his body so much that, in his darker moments, he had wanted to kill himself; in lighter ones he had wanted to leave his body behind and merge his mind to become part of a computer. He was sure that no one would ever desire his touch, no one would kiss him, no one would grasp his hand and take him to a place where they could undress each other in peace. He was sure that he would never wake up naked next to another naked person, never fall asleep with another person's back against his belly. He was sure that no one would ever say 'I love you' to him, that he would never say it to anyone.

Saharaflower's smile was sunny and her gaze open, her words easy to respond to. She sent pictures of the desert with waves like the sea, and the old town of Ghadames, on the roofs of whose white, lime-washed buildings only women had long ago been allowed to walk.

'There's always someone to say what girls can or can't do,' Saharaflower said. 'But when I have done what I am planning to do, they will be silenced for ever.'

There was something enticingly threatening about her words.

'What are you planning? he asked, feeling in his belly the buzzing of small flies.

'Can you keep a secret?'

'It's about the only thing I *can* do.'

'I like you.'

His finger paused above the keyboard. His breathing stopped. The fly crawling up the wall, the curtain fluttering in the breeze, the tram going by beneath the window, for a moment all of them stopped. He looked at his unmade bed, the dust in the corners of the room, the pale skin of his hand, the coffee stain on his trouser leg. He was alive and awake and that enchanting girl had said she liked him.

This is enough, he thought. *Whatever happens, I have experienced this moment. Life is not pointless.*

A sob rising to his throat made his breathing heavy; he wanted to write what he felt to the girl, how all-consumingly important her words were to him, but he realised that he could not do so, that it would reveal him completely, everything sad and pitiable about him, so he wrote quickly: 'Same here.'

Saharaflower told him about her family. Her father had died in battle against the country's former dictator and her brother in the civil war that had continued for more than a generation.

'People here have been waiting for something big ever since we got rid of G. The only big thing we got was massive chaos.'

'What's the cause of that?'

'Everything. Lust for power. Despair. Water. No one remembers anything else any more.'

'Water?'

'Drought. The groundwater has all been pumped away.'

'That's bad.'

'But not a surprise.'

'They never are.'

'Do you think what I think?'

'?'

'That everything has to change.'

'Of course. But how can it happen?'

'People must be awakened.'

'How?'

'With weapons.'

The buzzing flies in his belly turned into galloping horses. He had not been thinking of anything in particular. His mind had been filled with images of himself and Saharaflower hand in hand on the world's railways, sleeping outside beside a Finnish lake and in a tent in the Libyan Desert, organising demonstrations and living a nomadic life with plenty of lovemaking and talking, but nothing like ordinary life, family or money worries. In these images Saharaflower was the girl he had dreamed about since he was a child, a soulmate like a spirit being who would not demand anything and whose presence would create a place in the world for him too, a space in which he could look around him instead of staring in horror at his own violently detached and imperfect self.

As a child and a young man, images like these had been his refuge. When he had stood at break time beside the school wall wishing he could merge with the rough surface of the bricks, he had told himself a story about himself in unfamiliar countries with a girl, a soft-skinned, angel-like creature, who would grasp his hand and take him away from the gazes of other people. When, as he grew up, his body became awkward and smelled of medicines and when his future changed from an agonisingly endless place into a closed space, the power of the story vanished. There was only one reality, the joyless world in which he walked with the heavy steps of an outsider without the slightest interest in life, who had either to dare to put an end to himself or to continue to the end.

Now Saharaflower's bright eyes and sharp words returned the possibility of an alternative world to his mind with such force that it felt as if she were grabbing and shoving him towards the unknown with her slim, strong hand. He was ready to follow her anywhere; to do whatever it occurred to her to ask him.

'Tell me more,' he wrote, his fingertips flickering flames. 'I want to hear everything!'

'My cousin found two hundred bodies in the desert yesterday,' the girl wrote. 'Young men, women and children, a few babies bound to their mothers' backs. They had been lying in the sun for so long that they smelled. Some of them were almost completely covered in sand.'

'That's horrible.'

'It happens all the time. Hundreds of bodies are found in the desert or at the bottom of the sea. Before, everyone was horrified, but now no one takes any notice. It's enough that we ourselves survive. Do they end up on the news in your country?'

'The European refugees do.'

'The Africans don't?'

'Sometimes. If there's something special, a lot of children or something.'

'Well, of course. Guess what we think here?'

'Well?'

'The same as there.'

'In other words?'

'That Africans don't matter. That they're retarded idiots and that all they know how to do is reproduce.'

'But you *are* Africans.'

'If you say that here you will have your throat cut.'

'That wouldn't necessarily be a bad thing.'

'There's no unrest there?'

'Depends how you look at it. A bit of a spat in Greece and Spain. A few little incidents here, a few spats between Nazis and anarchists and some shootings.'

'And people who weren't there carry on as if nothing has happened?'

'Yes.'

'And from time to time there is some demonstration or civil action?'

'Or performance. A while ago there was an environmentalist street-theatre performance.'

'Street theatre?'

'A group of actors went round the streets of Helsinki dressed as Africans who had fled the drought.'

'And everyone realised that this is a really terrible thing and something has to be done?'

'Naturally. Sometimes of course there are attempts at something else. There are sit-ins at the airport and coal-fired power stations. A couple of politicians have been killed. And a little while ago the boss of an oil company was killed.'

'Do those things work?'

'No. People concentrate on grieving. And begin to go on about freedom, resistance to terrorism, how we won't be bullied. That shit.'

'Would you be prepared to do something bigger?

I would, he wanted to say. *I would be ready to blow up the whole world if you asked me to.* But he knew he should not sound enthusiastic. He had learned this from observing boys who had succeeded in getting close to girls. You can't be enthusiastic. You have to be cool.

'Depends what the aim is. Like I said yesterday, violence is the strongest political tool. It can only be used if your aims are such that they can be achieved by violence. Your aims have to be justified, and violence the only, or at least the most effective, way of achieving them. But what is justified is, of course, endlessly debatable. So in the end the decision is always with the perpetrator of violence.'

'I knew you would understand.'

Through the night they pondered the possibilities of violence. What could you achieve by killing as many well-off people as possible? They debated this theoretically and intellectually, as if they were talking about politics or economics. Nevertheless typing made his forehead sweat. He tried to imagine what it would feel like to see people falling and dying on the street, what it would feel like to do something like that. What it would feel like to do something like that together and at the same time as this unknown and amazingly familiar girl, what it would be like to prepare for the right moment alone and know that on the other side of the world the girl would be preparing for her own act at the same time. What that kind of connection with another person would be like.

The darkness of night deepened on the other side of the window. He had left the curtains open and now he saw his reflection in the glass, his slack posture and the body which could be beautiful if it were not covered in pale, lifeless skin, the result of endlessly changing medication and years in which he had built in the darkened room a nest which he did not wish to leave. He drew the curtains and covered all the reflective surfaces in the flat; the horrible ruin of his body should not be revealed, should not reveal him even to himself.

'I don't approve of the idea that killing should be some kind of statement. We need to have a concrete aim.'

'The culling of the human race.'

'?'

'We need to kill so many people that what we've done is visible and tangible. Nothing can continue as before.'

'How?'

'We'll recruit enough people. This needs to happen at the same time all over the world. It needs to be a kind of . . . global genocide. We need to start a movement that will continue after us. The aim is the culling of the human race until man can live in harmony with nature.'

39

Now he is a little boy who wants to sit on some-one's lap. His hand is clenched around the butt of the rifle; the cold chews at his bones and hunger at his belly. He longs for food so much that it hurts; something to warm his mouth and fill his stomach, something that tastes familiar.

'Do you want something?' asks the policeman sitting in the car below in a practised, calm voice.

'Could I have some food?'

'Food?'

'I'm terribly hungry.'

'If you put your weapon down.'

He releases his grip on the rifle again. Relief. The responsibility no longer rests with him. He presses his hand against his head, which is heavier than before; his whole body is heavy, a sodden sack, impossible to lift.

'Good. There's no need to panic,' the man below continues, and his voice is so ordinary and warm that he would like to climb down right now, to put his gun down and sit in the warm car next to the friendly policeman, to look at the empty city and talk about all sorts of things, as if there were endless time and no one had any need to panic.

'What would you like to eat?'

'Anything, as long as there's no meat.'

'Are you a vegetarian?'

'I am.'

'Why?'

'I don't accept that animals should be reduced to products.'

'You value animals?'

'I don't *value* anything.'

'Why, then?'

'Animals have an intrinsic value. Their value does not depend on what I or you think of them. Animals are living, sentient beings. It is sick for an intelligent, sentient being to be made into some kind of thinner-than-thin sliced ham.'

'What about people?'

'Are you trying to be clever?'

'Am I?'

'You're going to ask how I can think that animals have an intrinsic value but people don't. Or if people have intrinsic value, how can I want to shoot them.'

'Yes, I probably did think of asking that. Could you tell me what it is you do think?'

'I think that all living beings have an intrinsic value. But the well-off elite that holds economic and cultural power at the moment has, through its own actions, called its own intrinsic value into question.'

'Go on.'

'In just the same way as one can believe that individual freedom does not confer the right to limit the freedom of others, one can believe that the intrinsic value of living beings does not confer the right to exploit the value of other beings.'

'Do you mean the exploitation of animals by humans?'

'Not only that. I mean all the ways in which well-off people throughout the world exploit the possibility of a life of value not only of animals but of less well-off people and of the whole of creation.'

'How do they, or I am sure we, do that?'

'For a couple of generations we have indulged in a lifestyle in which it is normal both to treat animals as products and to consume natural resources at such a rate that it reduces the capacity of other people to live lives worthy of human beings all over the globe. Not to speak of the capacity of future generations to live here at all.'

'A vegetarian pizza's arrived,' says the policeman. 'Shall we go on talking once your stomach is full?'

'Fine. Thanks.'

'Will you come here to eat?'

He would like to say yes. He would like to leave it all, to leave his weapon on the roof and climb down, to look at the city through the window of the police car and hope that the world will always stay behind the glass running with raindrops.

'I can't . . .' he begins, and he can also see Saharaflower standing on the roof of her white-painted town, on a narrow ridge where you fall if you put a foot wrong and where, decades ago, only women were allowed. He sees Saharaflower, cool and confident, a scarf on her head and the diamond-decorated sunglasses shading her eyes, in the crosshairs of her Russian-made rifle, which has seen many civil wars, a bus from which Italian tourists are alighting.

'Could I have it here?'

40

Aava

'Darling, are you OK?'

I am sitting on the steps, my face against my knees, my arms around my legs. Gerard crouches in front of me. His breath smells of beer and marijuana and in his voice is the trace of an evening of impassioned conversations and black humour appreciated only by people living in the same situation. Behind Gerard the talk still bubbles.

'Come with us, G.?' Eva's voice asks from the midst of the darkness.

'Go on,' I whisper, my face still against my legs. 'As long as you get them away from me!'

Gerard strokes my arms. His hands are dry and warm.

'What did you say?'

'Go away. Please leave me alone.'

'I'm staying here,' Gerard says to the people standing a small distance away. 'Thanks for the company, it was a good evening.'

'Is there something wrong with Aava?' asks Eva.

'Just not feeling too good.'

'I hope no one she knows is—'

'No.'

'Can I do anything?'

'Good night.'

As their footsteps recede, Gerard strokes my neck and my back with strong caresses.

'You go too,' I whisper. 'Please go.'

Gerard continues with his caresses as if he has not heard me. He sits on the steps behind me and takes me in his arms with a force he has not used before.

Gerard takes me by the hand, pulls me up, takes me inside and turns on the light, pressing down on my shoulders to sit on the bed, takes the phone and reads the news and the message from Aslak that is visible beside it. He sits down next to me and does not ask anything, holding me close and caressing me more surely and decisively than before. I squeeze his wrist. At last my breathing resumes, the air flows through my nose to my diaphragm and out; my lungs, my belly, everything inside fills with air, grows lighter and returns to its correct place. Warm tears flow down my cheeks. Quietly, I stroke Gerard's hand.

'Let me be alone tonight,' I say again.

'I won't.'

41

Laura

'He was, or is, my favourite philosopher.'
'Nietzsche?'

'No. Serres. The one who he . . . who Aslak refers to in his video.'

The police officers are sitting opposite me. The wounds in my hands burn; I wrap new cold towels around them and return to the table. I do not want anything to change. As long as the police are here, as long as their tape recorder is on the table, as long as their dark-blue uniforms make the whole room darker, I will be all right.

'How much do you know about your son's ideology?'

I press my face into my hands for a second. The cold towels cool my eyes and my forehead. In my lectures Aslak's face was always serious, his posture more relaxed than elsewhere, as if he had found himself in the right place for a moment. He came orienteering with me in the forest, and we slept in the tent and looked at the stars in the evenings. In the forest we were silent for long periods together; it was a light and easy silence, and we walked at the same pace close to each other.

'At one point, while he was a schoolboy, he was very interested in what I did.'

'Which is?'

'I work for an environmental organisation. I specialise in climate politics.'

The police officers glance quickly at each other.

'The things he talked about in the video. Are they familiar to you too?'

The ice melts at the bottom of my stomach.

'I have never believed in violence.' My voice breaks. Of course. I am being accused. Every single moment, from this moment on, for the rest of my life, I will blame myself for what my son is doing now.

'I have always opposed violence. That is something I wanted to teach my children too. That violence can never, in any circumstances, be the solution.'

Almost twenty years ago a Norwegian man killed dozens of young people on an island where they had gathered to talk about politics.

'It was a political, rational act. Without question. It was unexpected, but perhaps not unexpected after all,' said the man's mother later. I read the book about the man's life as soon as it was published and was upset by it in a way I could not share with anyone. I thought about his mother – a woman who had died of cancer by the time the book appeared; the girl who had grown up in a poverty-stricken home fleeing her brother's blows and her sick mother, who hated her daughter. I had dreams in which the face of the gunman's mother turned into my face, his mother into a mother who walked behind me with her hand raised to strike me. Sometimes, as I got dressed to go to work, when I pulled on my neat clothes and the appearance of a confident person, I thought about that man's mother. The woman who wore clothes she could not afford and carefully coiffed her hair, and who was desperate to learn to behave as if she were one of them.

The policewoman takes a mouthful of water. She swallows and I can almost feel the cool water in her throat and her guts, behind her professional impassiveness a growing irritation as she waits for me to continue, the thoughts that force their way into her tired mind, the pansies growing in the garden, the smell of a sauna on the lake shore as it warms up, the nimble fingers of a random lover.

Ever since I was a child I have struggled to be one of the crowd. I have tried to become ordinary, a person who could do their share, who could, when something bad happens, follow it from the sidelines, grieve along with the other outsiders, be useful and serve others. And then go home, always finally go home and sleep an innocent sleep beside a loved one. I have decided to be the same as other people. I have decided to be a normal woman. When I was young, I hated the word ordinary, but once I had become pregnant I understood its power. When, at the health centre, I complained of pains and the nurse said everything was perfectly normal, I wanted to hug her. Before children, everyone probably wants to be unusual, an amazing person, and to live an unusual, amazing life. But as one gets older there is nothing more soothing than normality.

I struggled to be a normal mother. For us to be a normal family, our children normal children. A normal person has permission to take a break, permission to mingle with the crowd, permission to smile openly in the park and at parents' evenings, permission to believe that her child will keep up at nursery and at school, find friends, hobbies and dreams they can realise. I wanted to be a mother who has permission to believe that her child will, as an adult, come to lunch and will live long after I cease to exist.

I do not cry now, as it would feel excessive. Tears belong to people who are met with sudden injustice. They belong to people whose life is derailed by illness or accident, who have something that can be taken away. Tears are the privilege of people who expect something better. I don't cry, because I feel that this is what I deserve. What my child is doing at this moment is a naked and merciless reflection of me. His action reveals the darkness which I have tried to hide.

42

He sits on the roof with his eyes closed, his legs crossed and the palms of his hands held towards the sky as if he were meditating peacefully. The pizza beside him is cold and the box wet, the cheese melted into the cardboard. The policeman below is silent. The sniper aims at him from somewhere on high. Everyone is waiting to see what he will do. He thinks of cities he has not visited before, hot and cold, dry and wet, in different parts of the world, roofs sheltering people's homes, roofs onto which someone has now climbed, weapon in hand. He thinks about the girl with whom he planned all this, how deeply she must despise him.

The rule was that they should survive. They would all shoot as many people as possible before they were arrested, and if the police did not shoot them, they would not kill themselves. They would face their charges proudly and steadfastly, telling the court why they acted as they did and using every opportunity to persuade others to join them. They despise martyrs, and no one among them was to attempt to be one. They were political activists, ready to defend their aims and means in front of anyone; they knew the consequences of their actions and were ready to meet them head on. The rule was that on no account, in no circumstances, were they to kill themselves.

'Nothing is stupider than committing suicide,' said Saharaflower on his screen.

'Exactly. Not one of those clowns even wants to die. All they want is for someone to notice them,' he answered, closing another conversation which he had open at the same time, in which he had for years been discussing ways to commit suicide.

'It's the need for attention that makes people weak,' Saharaflower continued. 'No one who is dependent on others for attention can think clearly.'

As a child he liked to draw. He would sit quietly for hours, pencil and paper in front of him, concentrating so hard that he sometimes forgot to breathe, and when he finally exhaled the air he had held inside for a long time, Mum would crouch in front of him and stroke his head, asking anxiously if everything was OK.

Everything was fine then. He drew a world that he was able to create from scratch. It was a superworld in another solar system; its inhabitants looked like desert foxes, with big eyes and a friendly expression. In that world no one spoke, but everyone could read each other's thoughts. The plants, animals and desert-fox creatures, which were part human, part animal and alien, communicated with each other through tiny gestures, understanding each other without words, respecting the thoughts of others. It was a world of shared silence in which everyone had space to live freely, everyone had the right to be exactly who they were.

In the evenings as he waited for sleep he told himself stories about that world. And in the playground, first at nursery and then at school, as he followed the activities of the others, unable to join them, he imagined plants winding their way round the climbing frames, with silent desert foxes peeping out between them. For himself he imagined big ears, eyes and a tail which he could straighten; he could reach out his paws to the sky and fly towards another solar system and an unknown planet among whose inhabitants he would be at home.

The lives of all creatures are immeasurably valuable. That is what he wrote in his dairy on the evening when he refused to eat meatballs at Granny's house. Granny had insisted that he sit at the table until his plate was empty; he had heard Aava flitting through the flat in her fairy wings and watched the skin forming on the brown gravy until Mum had come to take them home.

'I don't want to eat animals,' he had explained to Mum, and Granny had looked on with a furrowed brow. Mum had helped him zip up his coat, ruffled his hair and said: 'It would be better if no one did.'

He cried in front of the television while watching a news item about Iraqi children whose small bodies were buried in a mass grave, and about Liberian children killed by the Ebola virus, whose bodies were covered with a blanket.

'What can I do?' he asked Mum and Dad. Together, they made a donation to the Red Cross and Christian Aid and considered what he might he study to get a job where he could change the world.

For a moment he dreamed of studying medicine and going to help children whose legs were as slim as tulip stems. He dreamed of the life that his sister now lives, helping unknown people far away from home. He thought that if he only waited long enough, something would change. He would learn to be at ease with other people, to take part in conversation and sometimes even to tell jokes. He would go to university and make the friends he didn't have at school. He would meet a girl with a friendly smile who might like him. And one day he would have a family and children; he would stroke them out of their nightmares and back to sleep and tell them there was nothing to be afraid of.

Gradually the exhaustion that he felt when he woke up every morning became so heavy that his whole life was dense and grey, a rag stinking of old food. The dreams he had had become someone else's dreams, someone who had the energy to get out of bed in the morning and join the other boys in the school playground.

'The lives of all creatures are immeasurably valuable.'

The voice is clear, delicate and serious, with a slight lisp. The voice is clearly audible, even though there is no one on the roof but him. It is a child's voice, that of a small, serious boy. A boy who believes that everything can get better.

PART FIVE

*For love is lonely,
lonelier than death.*

EEVA-LIISA MANNER
*Jos suru savuaisi
('If grief should smoulder')*

43

Cities

It is dry and hot. It is cool and dry, rainy and warm, mist and roofs covered in smog. It is completely clear. It is summer in Africa and autumn in Europe.

There is China, biggest of all; the United States, which is afraid; India, of whose riches nothing trickles down to those who were born in the wrong place. There is Europe, which is still waiting to join in.

There are streets swept by car headlights and streets where only stray dogs strut and a woman pale as smoke sweeps yesterday's rubbish. There are churches and minarets, flea markets and clubs, street food, delivery bikes and rickshaws driven by men with strong shoulders, strong gazes. There is a family moving house on a moped, complete with a granny and three canisters of water; there are open-top cars, sports cars and station wagons; there are cars with tinted windows, too big for small streets.

There are shacks built of tin and houses whose lawns are smooth and whose gardens are planted with carefully chosen flowers, and where no one dares open the door to a surprise visit from a friend. There are tall buildings and small buildings, four-lane motorways and alleys that no one has named. There are primary schools and private schools, Steiner schools, feminist schools, music schools and forest schools, little children on story mats they have made themselves and children whom no one expects home. There is a spot on a sandy beach where footprints walking together end in a soft dip with a forgotten hair clasp; there are sleeping bags in hollows in the road, in their openings faces that could belong to a child and beside them a dog with a trusting look and bare patches in its fur, its muzzle against its owner's hand.

There are organic brunches and vegan brunches, Korean, Chilean and Madagascan brunches; there are children flying kites in a pub garden and Japanese men who, waking up in a tent, put on a freshly pressed suit. There are cities where you can walk in safety through the night and those in whose well-kept streets only thieves walk. There are bridges which are slept under and bridges you can stop under to kiss. There are clubs that close their doors when the sun rises and clubs that open at the same time. There are concert halls and double-bass players in the street, jazz, rock and a little punk, a solitary woman singing an aria at the entrance to the station and a postman whistling 'What a Wonderful World'.

There is a slim-necked girl who hears she is to be married, flees into the night and throws herself under a train before her father and brother can do it for her. There is a woman who packs her own and her children's clothes into a tote bag, heart thumping, forgets her daughter's shoes and goes back to get them, meets a man on the stairs and never returns. There is a man who has a mark left by a ring on the fourth finger of his left hand who sits on a train long before it is due to depart and a woman sitting opposite him who asks to borrow a pen. There is an old woman who passes a man she loved when she was young in the street, watches a seagull peck at a potato chip and decides to turn round, running to catch up with the man even though her heart will not really let her run any more. There is a woman and a man, a man and a woman, a man and a man and a woman and a woman; there are things that are not spoken about and things that are shared, things that can perhaps be written about and things that are just somehow sensed; there are pictures that only one person remembers and shared moments that leave a different trace in everyone.

There are cities that everyone wants to visit and cities to which no one who has left them returns. There are building sites and ghost buildings, there are city blocks that have changed from desolate to comfortable and streets where the dust left by bombs still floats.

In all the cities, those of unhappy people and happy people, lonely people and people who are surrounded by friends, there is one person who is at this moment completely alone, and yet connected to the others. There are men and women dressed in dark clothes, beautiful and ugly, popular and lonely, expelled from school and best in their class, all young and so angry that it obscures everything else. Some have bought a weapon with money they have earned themselves and some have fetched an inherited weapon from a cupboard whose key has been easy to find. Some of them have decided to die, others to stay alive. Some want to take revenge on people they consider to have mistreated them, others just want revenge for its own sake; some want to make a dramatic exit and have their faces appear on television; some want an ex-girlfriend to remember them for ever; some really believe their deeds will change the world. Their hands are sweaty and their hearts pound. All of them are thinking, *Can I really do this?*

In Rio de Janeiro a young woman decides she can't, hides her weapon and buys a doughnut from a street stall. In London a young man decides he can't, hides his weapon and throws himself under a Tube train.

In other cities they proceed quietly, doubtfully, obstinately urging themselves to go to the place they have agreed on together. They hide, load their weapons, aim and begin to shoot.

44

'Is everything OK?' asks the policeman on the phone. The phone is still on, and the police officer has the voice of an old singer; he wants to give in and let it reassure him, the soft, gentle cadence.

'In this situation that's a slightly odd question.'

'It looks as if you're not doing very well.'

'Me? But I'm part of the well-off elite.'

'You've certainly kept your sense of humour.'

He would like to say something else, but the pressure in his belly intensifies so that he has to curl up in foetal position on the roof. The roof is cold and wet against his cheek; there is a ringing in his ears and his clothes are wet through. He breathes quietly but deeply, trying to get the pressure to ease so that his voice will be clear, so that he can say one sentence clearly and brightly. He is terribly tired and heavy, so tired that he can hardly move a limb. He closes his eyes and thinks about the desert foxes he drew as a child, the distant land where all life is valuable, where everyone has space to be quiet.

When he can breathe again, he sits up, squeezes the phone in his hand and says: 'Listen.'

'Yes?'

'It was good to talk.'

'Me too. What if we continued the conversation down here?'

'That would be nice.'

'I'll tell you how to come down.'

'Don't bother.'

'Why?'

'Please would you tell my parents and my sister something?'

'What have they got to do with it?'

'Will you promise?'

'I promise.'

'Tell them that nothing I have done has anything to do with them.'

45

Laura

When the police have gone, I call Aava. Uncharacteristically, she answers right away.

'Mum.'

'Sweetie.'

'I already know.'

For a long time we say nothing. I lean against the wall, close my eyes and listen to my daughter's breathing on the other side of the world.

When Aava and Aslak were children, I often woke in the night in terror that something had happened to one of them. I crept into their room, switched on the fairy and aeroplane night lights and looked at the sleeping children's smooth faces in their glow. I sat for a long time on the floor beside their beds. I stroked their cheeks, which were warm and soft as a rose petal, listening to their breathing and praying, I who have never believed in God, praying that nothing bad would ever happen to them.

'Have people . . . died?'

'I don't know yet.'

'How could . . . how could . . .?'

'Yes, sweetie.'

'Did you and Dad . . . did you have any idea?'

'I don't know. I think about it now all the time. Did we have any idea?'

'As soon as I heard that there was someone, I . . .' Aava's voice breaks.

'Sweetie?'

'If people have died, it's our fault. We all had an idea.'

I lean against the wall. My hand is carved from ice, cold and motionless.

'Darling, nothing is your fault. You are not responsible for your brother. Dad and I . . . we are guilty.' The face reflected in the window is at the same time my face and someone else's. For the first time in speaking to Aava I feel myself to be completely adult, capable of bearing responsibility.

'Mum.' Aava's voice is gentle. She would be a good mother. She would be much better than me. 'What's going to happen next?'

'I don't know.'

'How are you?'

'I don't know.'

'What are you and Dad doing?'

'Eerik is still on his way home.'

'What are you doing?'

'Waiting for Eerik. Breathing.'

'Do you want me to come back?'

The question surprises me. Since she left home, Aava has wanted to stay as far as possible from us. Even now I expected her to hang up the phone or shout at me, to tell me that she never wants to see us again.

For the first time in years it feels as if we are not fighting, but are on the same side, as close as it is possible for the two of us to be.

'What do you want, yourself?'

'Maybe I want to be here. To do the job I've agreed to do. It feels . . . it feels as if it's the only thing . . . I can do now.'

Aava gets her voice under control. I can almost see her straining to keep her posture straight and her face calm in order to be able to talk about this as she would about anything else, things that just happen.

'Then that is what you will do.'

I say it without bitterness. Too often, the envy I feel for Aava has crept in behind my words and twisted them to be different from what I intend. I have tried to be a loving mother and have ended up a bitter woman full of blame and controlled aggression.

Now the envy is gone. In its place is shame, a guilt the size of the whole of the rest of my life about each of my choices, each of my moments of incompetence and uncertainty, everything I have been as a mother.

The guilt is so massive and dense that it is difficult to see anything through it. At the same time I feel a momentary relief. I wish Aava well so sincerely, so profoundly, that it seems as if a limb that has been in the wrong position has finally clicked into place.

46

When Eerik comes home, he already knows. He opens the door and steps into the hall which the police left a moment ago. I walk up to him and we hug each other so tightly that it hurts. We sink to the floor against each other, Eerik still in his outdoor clothes, on his back the same worn rucksack that he takes on all his trips, I with wet towels still around my hands.

Eerik's face and neck have burned on his trip. The skin peels in thin rolls from his neck. I press my face against it and breathe in the smell of sand and the sun cream I packed for him. I hear the beating of his heart and feel the vein in his neck rising and falling against my cheek. I am grateful that he understands that it is better if he does not speak. That he does not try to ask anything and that he does not weep. I am grateful that he is here. That after all these years he is here, that he is holding me.

'I've got to get out,' I say finally.

Eerik nods.

'Maybe it isn't too late,' I say; I can almost believe it myself. 'Perhaps there is something we can do.'

We dress without speaking – thick shoes, woollen sweaters, waterproof coats. I take a big woollen scarf from the shelf and consider wrapping it round my neck so that, if necessary, it will also cover my face. The scarf is almost twenty years old. I bought it on a cycling trip in the archipelago when Aava and Aslak were children; I folded it as a blanket for them, and they fell asleep in the bike box with their helmets touching. I don't put the scarf on. I put it in a bag and take it to the rubbish bin in the yard; I slam the lid shut.

In the street in front of our building Eerik squeezes my hand. His grip is the same as always, his big hand around mine, the warmth of his palm against mine.

To the left of the door is the road Aslak and I walked along on his first day at school. The road he walked along alone later, a big backpack on his back, his eyes fixed to the ground. If he had looked back, he might have seen me glancing after him before I set off to work on my bicycle, looking as long as he remained in sight, as if nothing bad could happen to him as long as I could see him.

To the right leads the road we walked along to the playground and the rocks to have a picnic – me, Aslak and Aava – on evenings when Eerik was on a trip and I wanted to be a really good mother. I packed pancakes, blueberries and jam into a lunchbox, poured juice into a bottle and took the children out for supper. We played pirates, peering at passing joggers, scanning the sky for clouds that looked like animal heads.

Straight ahead is the road along which I cycled to lectures with Aslak, his big shirt fluttering in the wind, and hoped that that moment marked a new beginning.

If you go along that road and turn left you eventually come to the city centre, to the building on whose roof Aslak is now standing.

I am unable to look at Eerik. I cannot ask what he is thinking. The roads and rocks around us are full of memories of Aslak. From now onwards this will always be so. That child who, in the tram, points at passing cars. The parents who, in the restaurant, argue about whose turn it is to change a nappy. The gang of boys in the bus on a school trip, the jokes of the others, and one with a forced smile to show that he is present.

I don't know whether we will ever be able to talk about it. I don't know whether we will be able to go on living together, waking up in the same bed, seeing the pain in the other's face. But I do know that we will both go on living. For Aava's sake we will go on. We will stay alive to be there for her, even if she does not ask anything of us.

We do not set out until the door behind us opens. We walk hand in hand away from the building; we do not turn to see who came out.

We walk towards the centre of the city, an area that is cordoned off, quiet, because of our son. Eerik's stride is much longer than mine; I have to quicken my pace to keep up with him. He notices and slows down, squeezing my hand a little harder. We find a joint rhythm and walk, unspeaking, our collars shielding our faces, in the empty streets towards the building on whose roof Aslak is standing.

When Aslak was a few weeks old, we walked the same streets, all four of us, Aava on Eerik's shoulders and Aslak in a sling against my breast, his thumb in his mouth like a baby monkey. It was a windy day and I was wearing Eerik's big coat, inside which Aslak could take shelter. I could feel the baby's breath against my skin, the wriggling of the little body as he sought a good position to fall asleep. I wrapped the coat around him, pulling the zip up just far enough for him to have space to breathe and so that my hand could stroke his cheek. With my forefinger I caressed the soft down of Aslak's skin, feeling a love that made everything inside me tingle.

I saw the outlines of the buildings more sharply than before, heard the sounds of the city more loudly.

I will protect you from all of this, I thought as the tram rattled towards us, a bewildered-looking man broke an empty liquor bottle against the rubbish bin and a little boy lagged behind his friends. *I will carry you in my arms until you grow strong and tough enough to face all of this, to step into the world and to change it.*

I push a hand under my coat and can almost feel a baby's soft cheek against my finger, Aslak's face, whose thoughtful expression remained the same throughout the years.

I loathe the term working at grief. As if grief really could be something that you can survive with the aid of work, as if you could process the grief away and live without its scars and traces. It is the same kind of deception as the anti-wrinkle creams and cosmetic fillers you inject into your face. As if, some-where, there really was a substance that could turn time back, make our skin smooth again and our souls carefree, as if, by working hard enough, we could stay eternally young and enthusiastic, for ever believing that everything is possible for us.

Eerik and I are not working at our grief. We have no reason to break out of our grief, not a single reason to liberate ourselves from grief. Our only alternative is to carry it with honour, the weight of our own mistakes, of our own grief, of the love we have for Aslak. We will stay alive and love him. And every single day, as long as there is anything left of our memory, we will think about what we did wrong.

Our steps quicken as we approach the area blockaded by the police; the rhythm of our breathing quickens. We squeeze each other by the hand and run, so fast that are unable to speak even if we wanted to, towards the cordoned-off area at whose edges we can see the outlines of the army tanks.

47

He has always been a clumsy boy. The one who couldn't make a catch at baseball and who ran more slowly than the others.

Now he gets up, lithe as a cat, stepping onto the edge of the roof with one certain and easy stride. The lights of the police cars flicker in blue waves on the ground. He jumps before he has time to think about anything, head first as if he were diving into warm water swarming with silver-flanked fish.

48

Aava

I wake in yesterday's creased clothes, the pattern of the pillowcase on my cheek, in my mouth the taste of yesterday's dinner. Gerard is sleeping with his arms flung out; he too is wearing his day clothes, the stubble blue on his chin. I rest my hand on his ribcage, my palm against the peaceful beating of his heart.

I open the curtains I have hung on the narrow window. The sky is cloudless. The moon casts its pale glimmer into the room, the stars like holes leading to another, brightly lit world. I think of Bahdoon's grandfather gazing at the stars, waiting for the growing season to begin and for the children's arms to grow strong again.

A plane is will be waiting for me at Mogadishu International Airport in half an hour. The plane is a rusty Cessna; as I get in I always have sticky palms but a smile on my face. I have not told anyone here that I am afraid of flying. I wouldn't have the nerve to say anything like that.

The shower block is on the other side of the yard; at this time there may already be a queue. I clean my armpits and my face with a wet wipe; this time, it will have to do. Gerard's forehead is sweaty. I also clean his face; he murmurs in his sleep and pulls me closer. I press my face for a moment against his sleepy neck.

I pack a pen and notebook, bars of chocolate as snacks, and the lunch I ordered from the kitchen yesterday, a penknife, a water bottle and a walkie-talkie, and dress as I always do when I am going to the villages. Ugly underwear, an ankle-length skirt and over it a bulletproof vest, on my head a scarf which covers both my hair and most of the bullet-proof vest, and on top of the scarf a helmet. I pull soft socks onto my feet and on top of them sturdy hiking boots in which I can walk long distances in thick scrub. As I tie the laces my hands are shaking. I think about another young doctor, a Norwegian man, whom al-Shabaab kidnapped from a village health centre seven years ago and whose eyes still change when he talks about it.

'On field trips you have to remember that you can be kidnapped at any moment,' he said, and at the end of the sentence his voice began to shake.

'Wear proper shoes. If you're kidnapped you have to walk a lot.'

I pull my shoelaces into a knot by mistake; when I tug it just gets tighter. Tears flow down my cheeks;

I wipe them away with the edge of the scarf, cut the lace with a knife and tie the tangled lace. The front of the shoe gapes open so that there is no support for the ankle when I walk. If I were to be kidnapped on this trip, I would walk more slowly than the others. I would trip on roots and I would be weak. A weak victim makes kidnappers use harsher violence. A weak victim is easier to kill.

Before, I did not fear kidnapping. As I set off on this trip I thought about the war, which had been going on for so long that killing people had become easy. I thought about the roadside bombs, the kidnappings and the masked men who might attack residential areas in the middle of the night, kill the guards and do to the residents whatever would cause the most fear. I curled up on the sofa, drank tea, and thought a lot about what fear-hardened people who wanted to make foreign workers so fearful that they would no longer come here might do to me. I went through it all in my mind. *I want to do something good in places where no one really wants to go*, I had written in my journal back then. *It is the only thing that makes sense in my life. If the cost is to be killed or raped, I am prepared to pay it.*

A news item glows on the screen of my phone. I glance at it once more.

Danish terrorist arrested for planning attacks

In simultaneous attacks in New York, Shanghai, Helsinki, Gothenburg, St Petersburg and Ghadames, Libya, 46 people were killed and 283 wounded. According to police the figures may rise, for some of the wounded are in a critical condition. Five people have been arrested on suspicion of murder. Three of the accused have committed suicide.

Twenty-seven-year-old Lauri Aslak Anttila carried out the Helsinki attack.

Lars Skovgaard Jensen, who has been arrested in Libya, is suspected of masterminding the attacks. Forty-three-year-old, Danish-born Jensen is one of the world's most wanted terrorists. He spent his youth in neo-Nazi circles in Denmark and influenced the radicalisation of the far right in Denmark. Subsequently he has lived in Iraq, Ukraine and Libya and participated in many terror attacks with both far-right and Islamist groups. The police are silent on the question of whether Jensen's acts are informed by any unifying ideology. Jensen is known to participate in internet chat groups under many assumed identities. He communicated with Anttila in the guise of a woman under the alias Saharaflower.

I quit the news item. In my mind is a thick door and in it a lock which no one can open. Behind the locked door is Aslak.

Now all I think of is the journey I must undertake. The coming days, weeks and years, when I must stay in this country and focus on being able to do something, at least.

I pull the covers over the sleeping Gerard, pull a piece of paper from my notebook and write: *Thank you.*

Outside it is cool. At the edge of the dark-blue sky the pale red strip of morning is spreading. In this city I love most of all this moment, when the pale, warm light fans the night into morning and the antennae rising from the buildings are outlined against the glowing sky. The city is for a moment so quiet that near the sea you can hear the sound of the waves. You can close your eyes, smell the salty air and imagine that the day contains the promise of something good.

Bahdoon is at the door. He is reading a newspaper and brings dark tea, raising his eyes and smiling when he sees me.

'Sister. How are you?'

I put my bag down on the ground, sit on it and press my hands to my face.

An armoured car will be coming to fetch me soon. The plane will take off shortly. It will land on a runway the width of its wheelbase cleared from the dense brush; the guard will announce on his walkie-talkie to the group that controls the village that I am about to arrive, and the nurse will come and meet me. Before I can start work, I must meet the chief and the village elders – wise-eyed, orange-bearded men who thank me for coming and offer me warm lemonade, which must be drunk. After that it is time for what I like most: measuring the children's arms in the health centre with the local nurse. Talking to these calmly working women in the simple but neat and systematically functioning health centre in a mud hut always reassures me.

I admire the serenity with which the women do their jobs despite the fact that the local doctor was shot in this village a few weeks ago. The women's capacity to go on with their work despite these conditions puts the world back to rights for a moment. Work must be done. Whatever happens, work must be done.

'My brother . . .' I whisper to Bahdoon from behind my hands.

Bahdoon has never touched me. Now he takes me by the hand, pulls it gently away from my face and gives me a hot cup of tea.

'Drink this,' Bahdoon says. 'The car is ready.'

The mug warms my hands, the drink my mouth, chest and belly. I give the empty mug to Bahdoon and thank him, swallowing my tears, when he takes my hand again, a quick squeeze that conveys a sympathy that is too strong.

I get into the car where the guard is already sitting, a rifle on his shoulder.

When I decided to study medicine, I separated myself from Aslak. For years I dreamed about knives which cut Siamese twins apart from each other, amputated a hand or a foot, slashed a sternum open and dug out a still-beating heart. I had decided to go. I had decided to tear myself away from the past by violent means if necessary and to direct myself towards a life that suddenly seemed inviting and fresh, like a sea breeze in a stuffy room. I spread my arms and walked steadily in its direction; I no longer wanted to die, but to live.

'How can you abandon me like this?' Aslak asked, and I didn't have an answer. He appeared in my dreams and in quiet, solitary moments; my memories were Aslak's memories and my shadow Aslak's shape. I could not tell Aslak anything about it. I could not tell anyone else, could not explain what is was like for another life to walk alongside my own life, the person I loved the most, in whose life nothing had ever begun, and how that person's world was much more real than mine.

Some time later, perhaps a very long time later, I think about Aslak again, my little brother, who used to creep under my covers to sleep. Now all I think about is work.

I think about women who bury their husbands and children and go on working. Women who are not afraid of gunshots, machetes or rape. Women who go to work and do their jobs well, asking everyone how they are, filling in their health records, joking with the little patients resting in the corner of the mud hut, using humour to create, in the health centre and the surrounding village, an atmosphere of quiet hope. The women work showing that it is possible to do this too, to continue working even though everything around has been destroyed, to continue work which sustains order and hope, to demonstrate to people who encounter death every day that they are important. Amid endless violence there is nothing more important than to champion the meaning of life, all the more tenaciously, the more frustrating, hopeless and desolate it seems.

Bahdoon opens the gate and waves at me. I wave back. The call to prayer echoes over the city. The driver takes me to the airport. There the rusty plane awaits me, as ever.

Turn over for a sneak peek at *The Cleaner*
by Elisabeth Herrmann

1

It was not a good place to die.

Judith Kepler pulled the handbrake and turned off the motor. She watched the grey tenement building through the windscreen of the van and felt her stomach contract. Her palms, clinging to the steering wheel, were moist. And to top it off, she had an absolute beginner with her this morning.

Along the busy street there were rows of discount chain clothes stores, brothels and shady used car salesmen. A district where everything could be had on the cheap: women, cars, even apartments. Several of the building's windows were boarded up. In others, blankets and towels took the place of curtains.

Her front-seat passenger looked longingly at a rundown Ford Fiesta that could be driven off the lot for the monthly payment of only ninety-nine euros. Provided you had a steady job. Kai had neither ninety-nine euros, nor a job. He was a broad-shouldered, tall boy with a stylish Beatles haircut with the fringe combed into his face. It lent something unintentionally poetic to his powerful features, something he probably had no clue about. She flipped down her sun visor and looked into the mirror. What did twenty-one-year-olds think about women over thirty? They didn't even come into consideration, probably. She brushed back a strand of hair and at the same moment thought how vain she must seem to him. She did it every time she went onto a job site: hands washed, hair combed. First impressions mattered. That was true for apartments, jobs, men, and everything else that had to be taken care of properly.

Kai tore his gaze from the Ford Fiesta, raising his eyebrows all the way up to his fringe and asked sullenly, 'We going up there now or what?'

You'll be talking differently by the end of the first shift, Judith thought to herself and tried to keep a straight face.

She got out. Behind her back, she heard him do the same. He followed her like a puppy. He would probably turn on his heels as soon as he registered what he had got himself into, so she might just as well treat him with consideration in advance.

By the main entrance to the building the penetrating smell of urine reached their noses – an unmistakable sign that the night crawlers had taken over this part of the metropolis and marked their territory here. The door was 1950s hideous with an aluminium frame and security glass with multiple fractures. It was opened from the inside. An employee from the funeral home stepped out and locked the doors. He nodded briefly to Judith.

'Man, oh man.' He reached into his jacket pocket and extended a small metal tin. The gesture was a silent summary of what awaited her upstairs.

'Thanks.'

Judith rubbed the menthol cream under her nose. Then she passed the tin to Kai, who sniffed at it and gave it back. He hadn't graduated from school; the employment agency had told him this internship was his last chance. He had showed up at eight thirty instead of seven, mumbling some vague excuse about a broken alarm. The fact that he was still along for the ride was only because the doctor they were due to meet there had had an emergency and Judith had been forced to wait. And because Judith might be the only one at Dombrowski Facility Management who knew how alarms worked. She had four. Distributed throughout the apartment at strategic points, all hard to reach, and programmed to ring one minute apart. The last one was in the bath.

'Take it.' Judith offered him the tin again.

But Kai either didn't get it or considered menthol cream kid's stuff. His choice. Judith returned the tin to the mortuary assistant. He gave her a brief nod and lit himself a cigarette while casting a glance at the summer sky, which was just freeing itself from the hazy morning.

'Six weeks under the eaves, in this weather. We're just happy we managed to get her into the box in one piece.'

They knew each other. Not well enough to know the other's name. But in the way that at some point you get to know everyone who works in this strange profession: the administration of death. Everyone has their place. The doctor, who issues the death certificate. The undertaker, who picks up and arranges the corpse. The cleaner, who makes the house inhabitable again. They had a utilitarian mode of communication, eschewing all the fake half tones of lamentation and concentrating on the essentials: the job.

Kai turned even paler than he already was. The nice caseworker at the agency apparently hadn't prepared him for this. Facility cleaning. Scouring. Anyone can do it. Go there and take a look. And then this, right on the first day. Scuffling steps approached. The doctor, recognisable by his assiduous haste and a bulky leather bag, came down the stairs. He was followed by two rapid-response police officers.

'We're finished up there.' Like so many members of his guild, he referred to himself in the plural. 'Natural cause of death, passed away peacefully. My God.'

Two semi-trailers rumbled by. The physician stepped onto the wide footpath and inhaled a lungful of the ammonia and diesel mix. Then he shook his head and rushed to his car. The two officers followed him. The mortician was smoking.

'Then let's go.' Judith made the motion with her head that people use to command dogs into the house when it's raining. Kai trudged behind her.

They climbed the stairs. There were buggies in the hallway, shoes and clutter. Every storey got them further away from the street noise and closer to forgetting. Judith smelled the sweet hint of death in spite of the menthol. Six weeks, the man had said. And the only thing the neighbours had finally noticed was the stench.

Kai panted.

'What smells so bad?' he asked, but he had already guessed the answer.

Judith didn't intend to go easy on him. Whoever came along with her had to be ready to push their limits further than they wanted to. The public health department had called Dombrowski Facility Management. And Dombrowski had sent Judith. And Judith wasn't one to wrap rookies in cotton wool.

'This way.'

A narrow hallway with a threadbare runner, old wallpaper, winter coats in the wardrobe despite it being the height of summer. The first impression was that of poverty and meanness. This had dominated the life of Gerlinde Wachsmuth.

And the solitude, Judith thought as she entered the bedroom. There was a simple wooden cross hanging over the narrow bed. The second assistant mortician was just closing the zinc casket and was doing so with special care. Even the staircase was cramped; they would have to transport the corpse upright at some spots. His colleague returned from his cigarette break. The two stood next to the casket, folding their hands and murmuring a quiet prayer.

Judith asked herself if they also did that when there were no witnesses nearby. She was just about to give Kai a sign that, in keeping with the situation, he should also conduct himself reverently when she noticed the expression on his face. He stared past her, looking at the bed. His lower lip began to tremble. He swallowed frantically, his Adam's apple bouncing up and down his strong throat like a rubber ball. He clapped his hand in front of his mouth and lurched out of the room.

'His first time?'

The two had finished their prayer. Judith nodded. She looked at her watch and hoped Kai would vomit quickly. They had already lost a lot of time. But the sounds that emanated from the bathroom sounded more like an extended coughing fit. He was more likely avoiding work rather than having a true emergency. She would have liked to send the boy straight home. The wheat separated from the chaff at the bathroom door.

'I'm going to start,' she called. 'It'll all be subtracted from your lunch break.'

An argument that often worked wonders with people like Kai. Maybe someone should have advised him not to eat anything before this assignment.

First she examined the bed and the state of the mattress. It was positioned with the headboard against the middle of the wall. Pillows and covers were on the floor to the left, the casket was to the right. The only thing left of Gerlinde Wachsmuth was the impression of her body on the sheet. She must have been a small person, who lay down to sleep and didn't get back up. A silent death. A peaceful, expected departure. A quiet exit. Judith felt the peace and the absence of fear. Sometimes death was the only friend who wouldn't forget you.

And then Gerlinde Wachsmuth's corpse had had six weeks to dissolve during high summer in a poorly insulated apartment on the fifth floor. The silhouette of her body was a soft yellow, where her arms, legs and head had lain. But the shade darkened towards the middle of the body, almost reaching a dark violet, nearly black colouration. White dots were moving in the middle of the dark hollow.

Judith didn't have to look under the bed to know that fluid had collected underneath, contaminating the air. Although the assistant mortician had opened the window and the menthol cream burned on her upper lip, this smell burned its way into her pores like a sandblaster.

The two men lifted the casket and carried it out of the apartment as carefully as possible. Judith waited until she heard the toilet flush.

'Everything OK?' she called down the hallway.

The door opened. Kai emerged, staring at her with the *I want to go home* look everyone had the first time they saw behind the pleasant façade of how everything meets its end.

'I need safety goggles, a full-body suit. Disinfectants and cleaners. Cling film. A spray can, formaldehyde steamer, thermal and cold-process foggers. The locked poison box – larvicide, acaricide, phosphine and hydrocyanic acid. And of course the boxes with the scouring powder, hard soap, brushes and scrubbers. Understand?'

Kai shook his head.

'It's all in the back of the van.'

Instead of answering, he stumbled back into the bathroom and slammed the door behind him. Judith counted down from ten and waited. The gagging receded. Of course she could have gone down herself. But she didn't want to.

'Are we almost ready now?' She looked at her watch. 'I'll give you exactly one minute. Then I'm calling Dombrowski and telling him he should pull you.'

She could hear the toilet flushing, shortly followed by the sound of a tap splashing. When Kai opened the door for the second time, she turned around, expecting his departure.

'Got something for my nose?' he asked.

'Respirator mask.'

'Two, if possible.'

Judith grinned and pulled two out of her trouser pocket.

'There we are. Never go without.'

Judith bent down in front of the bed. Like Kai, she wore paper overalls, and rubber gloves reaching her elbows. She motioned to the spot that had spread out on the carpet.

'Chlorine and oxygen. But you still never get rid of the stench. The carpet has to go. If you're lucky there's a wood floor underneath that can be sanded.'

She stood up. Kai was still staring at the white dots in the middle of the mattress. They had stopped moving after Judith had sprayed them with larvicide. She removed her respiratory mask.

'Maggots. Seen with a little love, they're just another of God's creatures. At least they were. Cling film?'

'Wait . . . just a sec.'

Kai trudged into the hall and came back with the heavy roll. Luckily enough, Gerlinde Wachsmuth had passed away on a single bed. The mattress wasn't heavy. But the noise caused by some of the maggots falling onto the plastic they had spread out was causing Kai problems. It was like a handful of raisins.

'Is it always so disgusting?'

'No,' she lied. 'Usually you just have to strip the beds and clean up thoroughly.'

This was relatively harmless. Cleaners were regularly confronted with much worse. He was probably still here so he could tell his friends about this freak show, and how he was allowed to dart across the screen once as an extra. Wow, maggots. Corpses. Undertakers. Call me a hero. Judith removed the carpet knife from the toolbox and cut the rest of the plastic to length.

'Man, what kind of job is this? Why do you do it?'

She thought for a second. Given the lack of young people entering the profession, telling the truth probably wasn't advisable.

'Because I can. And lots of others can't.'

She cut off the last piece of plastic, retracted the blade and went towards the wide-open window. The midday sun had spread over the city like a bell jar. You could see the autobahn from here. She admired the symmetrical semicircles of the on and off ramps, over which the avalanches of metal rolled. The best view was from the TV tower. Sometimes Judith treated herself to a trip to the observation platform. Then she stared down at the city from above and was overcome by its restless beauty. She thought about how she wanted to drive out to the Lusatia region with a telescope tonight, searching for the ultimate dark spot, the place with the lowest levels of light pollution. She wanted to finally see a really starry sky again. August. The weeks of the Perseids, the meteor showers, granting the eternally hopeful human race a multitude of promises in the form of shooting stars.

She unzipped her overalls and removed a small pack of tobacco where she always kept a few cigarettes she had rolled beforehand. She offered Kai one of the crooked sticks.

'How did you know you could?' he asked. 'Did you do a suitability test at the job centre?'

He gave her a light. She leaned forward and saw his hands, which he held up, protecting the flame. They were young hands, with narrow fingers and big knuckles. Ten years more, and they would be the hands of a man. She inhaled the smoke and blew it past him, towards the window. He would understand in ten years, at the earliest.

'There are jobs you don't apply for. They come to you.'

'Just like that?'

'Maybe you don't get it yet. This here is a chance.'

Kai rested his forearm on the windowsill and looked like he wanted to give himself a little more time to think about it. They stood shoulder to shoulder, and the only sounds came from the traffic noise down below and the quiet rustling of their overalls. They smoked, and Judith blinked at the bright daylight and counted down the years separating them. She arrived at eleven. He was too young for everything that could cross your mind on a day like this, when the sweltering heat brought the blood in your veins to a boil and you suddenly thought about shooting stars in a dead person's apartment. She stubbed out her cigarette on the outer windowsill, donned her mask, which didn't make any noticeable difference, and went back into the room. Five minutes of fresh air had been enough to forget the stench of hell. It hit her like a sucker punch.

'And the deceased?' He wouldn't let it go. 'How do you deal with the dead?'

'We don't have a close personal relationship, if that's what you mean.'

Of course he didn't mean that. She sounded as callous as one of the doctors from those American television series that ran around the clock on cable. But it simply came down to the fact that for her, humans remained human, even after dying. They were given one last show of respect.

They walked up to the bed from either side. Kai bent over and lifted the mattress on one side, she from the other.

'I've never seen a corpse.'

'Won't be too long.'

'Maybe you should have become a cop, if you like dead people so much.'

The mattress fell to the ground. 'The door's over there,' she said.

Kai's eyes widened, staring at her in disbelief.

'I'm serious. You can go.' She reached for the roll with the tape, which she had put on the nightstand. 'I don't want to work with people like you.'

'What do you mean by that?'

'Just what I say.'

Kai cast an indecisive glance toward the hallway, the path to freedom, and an easy afternoon at the beach bar.

'And what will you tell the boss?'

She ripped off half a metre of tape, cutting it with her teeth because she didn't want to ask Kai for the carpet knife.

'That you're a fucking idiot.'

'What do you mean?'

Judith wasn't the slightest bit inclined to explain that to him as well. She folded the plastic sheet over the mattress, but the tape got tangled. Kai squatted down next to her and had the sheet under control with two quick steps.

'Sorry,' he said. 'Won't happen again.'

She furiously ripped off another piece of tape, extending it towards him. He cut it in the middle. They worked together in silence the next couple of minutes.

Judith started to sweat. Even if it was from a single bed, sealing the mattress was not an easy task in this weather. The overalls were like a sauna, and the mask didn't exactly help you breathe.

'I actually meant – you're a woman . . .'

'What does that have to do with anything?'

'What do you tell guys when they ask you what you do?'

'Depends if I want to get rid of them or not.'

She could tell from the look in his eyes that he was smiling. He was probably hoping it wasn't so bad after all.

She turned the mattress so Kai could make a clean rotation with the tape. The tape ripped, the sheet slipped out of her hands, and the mattress went straight over the nightstand, knocking off everything that had been on top. Glass shattered. Judith stifled a curse. There was a commandment that couldn't be broken: leave an apartment clean but undamaged. Kai bent over.

'Just a picture frame. And the light bulb from the lamp.'

'Put it back up.'

She took the frame off his hands. The glass had cracked. A photograph of a man aged around thirty was trapped behind it. The faded colours betrayed that the picture must be at least two decades old. She carefully removed the shards of glass from the wood and returned the frame to the night stand.

'What are you doing?'

Judith spun round. She hadn't heard the man coming, but his tone of voice and the first visual impression were a match. He was thin, almost gaunt, and the unhealthily red face revealed that he was either suffering from the stairs or was an alcoholic. A glance at his jaundiced eyes suggested that the latter was more likely. She discerned a vague, almost caricature-like similarity with the man in the picture.

'Hello. We've been assigned to de-putrefy the apartment.'

'What?'

'De-putrefy. The opposite of putrefy.'

'Not by me. Get lost.'

'According to the federal infectious disease laws, this apartment has to be properly cleaned and disinfected. I don't know if you're qualified to do it.'

'I'm not paying. Just so you know right now. What were you doing with my mother's nightstand? Don't think I didn't see you messing around with it.'

His gaze flitted around the room, coming to rest on the wrapped mattress.

'And leave that here. Don't touch a thing, you understand? Otherwise I'll call the police.'

'Was that your mother who was lying here for six weeks?' Judith removed her rubber gloves. 'My condolences.'

'Get out of here. Immediately.'

Kai took a step towards the man. Judith reached for his arm, but immediately let him go.

'No. You go,' she said. Her hand was still thinking about that contact, but her head blocked out the thought of the touch. 'I can't permit you to be here until we have finished.'

The man hadn't counted on resistance. Only now did he notice the changed chemistry of the room. He inhaled sharply through his nose. With remarkable transformational power his face revealed exactly what he felt: surprise, recognition, disgust.

'What's going on?'

'Your mother's body was picked up two hours ago. The funeral home will get in contact with you. You don't look as if you've made a long journey. So stop playing the doting son and let us do our work.'

'She's dead,' the man repeated. 'The people next door said that.'

He turned around and left. They heard sobbing from the living room.

Judith instructed Kai to bring the mattress to the car. While he was gone, she began to disinfect the room.

The use of further poisons wasn't necessary – the decay hadn't spread that far yet. Every time she fought her way through the narrow hallway into the bathroom she saw the man sitting on the couch, bent wide over as if he was searching for something on the threadbare carpet. On the fourth or fifth time she stopped and watched him. He wasn't looking for anything. He was just moving with the erratic motions of an addict.

'We're almost done here,' she said.

The man looked up.

'I have no one else left.'

Judith shrugged her shoulders. She didn't want to be sucked into a conversation.

'I know what you're thinking,' the man said. 'I should have taken better care of her. And you're right. Yes. You're right.'

He started to rock back and forth. She went back into the bathroom and filled a bucket with water. Of course she was right. But it wasn't her business to judge what had gone wrong in the life of Gerlinde Wachsmuth and her son. His photograph had stood next to her bed. He had been in her life but she wasn't in his. It was that simple and brutal. The old rage boiled up in her, but she had learned to keep it under control. You had to differentiate between what was right, what was necessary, and what was pointless. It was absolutely pointless to tell men like him the truth. It would roll off him like drops of rain on a dirty pane of glass.

She turned off the tap and then went back to the bedroom without wasting another glance on the hypocrite in the living room. A little later Kai joined her and they worked until the early afternoon without looking up once.

Judith slipped out of the overalls and stuffed them in the blue bin bag. Her work was done. She was satisfied. She instructed Kai to carry the sacks of rubbish down and followed him into the hallway.

'Mr Wachsmuth?'

The door to the living room was closed. She opened it and uttered a quiet sound of surprise. Kai, already almost outside, turned around and came back to her.

'It can't be true,' was all he said.

The doors of the living room cupboard had been ripped open. The drawers had been pulled out, their contents spread out across the floor. Several picture frames were scattered carelessly on the tiled coffee table. Their backs revealed that someone had searched for something with great haste and little care. Light-coloured spots on the wallpaper glowed where they had hung. Judith lifted one of them. It was a poor facsimile of Spitzweg's *The Poor Poet*.

'The pig is gone.' Kai, having inspected the entire apartment once again, returned. 'What now?'

Judith held the print in front of a spot that would have been the right size.

'We have to clean up.'

She put the picture to one side, kneeled down, and started to refill the drawers. Shot glasses, shoehorns, half-burnt candles, lace doilies, a box of photos. All had been tossed to the ground, spread across the floor all the way to the couch. Kai sighed, picked a cushion off the ground and fluffed it repeatedly.

'If I ever see that guy again . . . First he leaves the old woman to rot and then he steals from her.'

'Gerlinde,' Judith said. 'The old woman's name is Gerlinde Wachsmuth.'

She was holding a photo of a man, a woman and a child. Taken sometime in the sixties, when people still assumed a pose in front of the camera, but were no longer spruced in their Sunday best. The man was broad-shouldered and rather stout. Although he gazed sternly into the camera, he had draped his arm around the woman's shoulder. There was an almost girlish smile on her round face. The boy's lower lip protruded. He looked up to his father and grinned at him.

Judith flicked through the remaining photos in the box. The man appeared several more times. The child developed into an ugly teenager with sideburns and long hair and began to assume a similarity to the wreck that she had encountered in this apartment a couple of hours before. Then the man disappeared. The woman appeared a few more times, posing in front of the Eiffel Tower or on a beach boardwalk. The rest were portraits cut out from passport photo machine prints.

A pictorial history of the pursuit of a little happiness. Father, mother, child. A family. Not perfect. Rather pathetic even, when the son goes as far as to steal from his dead mother. But Judith had a weakness for families. She pocketed the photo. The box would land on the rubbish heap anyway, just like everything else from the old woman's belongings that couldn't be turned into cash.

'Are you swiping something?' Kai had rehung *The Poor Poet* and was straightening it.

'Not really. I collect family photographs.'

'Don't you have any of your own?'

'No.'

Kai must slowly be getting the message that her sense of humour was limited. But he had learned enough today to know when it was better to keep his trap shut.

The heat tasted like burnt rubber. When Judith opened the driver's door, it felt like she was climbing into an oven. Despite taking the autobahn, she needed almost an hour to get to Neukölln. The rush hour traffic was stop-start in both directions. The further south she went the more frequently she was passed on the shoulder by low-riders with tinted windows and boots full of subwoofers. She wiped sweat from her forehead and rolled up her long sleeves.

Kai had fallen asleep on the passenger side. His head lolled against the side window, the exhaustion so extreme that not even the potholes roused him from his coma. She risked a second glance. Did everyone get so tired at that age? She tried to remember how she had felt when she was that young. But she only ran into a blazing flame of self-hatred, vague yearning and depressing despondency. She saw the scars on the crook of her arm and rolled her sleeves back down.

Kai only jolted upright when she reached Dombrowski's headquarters and turned off the motor. She motioned to a pockmarked steel container rusting away next to the entrance.

'That's where the rubbish goes. Your job.'

She removed the key and tossed it to him. He was still too groggy to react and let it fall to the ground.

'Should I come on Monday?'

'Do you want to?'

'I have to think about it.'

He searched for the key. She had already got out by the time he had found it and resurfaced.

'Hey!' he called after her.

Judith didn't turn around. She raised her hand in a fleeting parting gesture and walked across the dusty asphalt to the old tyre storage that her boss had converted into an approximation of a real company headquarters. There were lockers, showers, changing rooms and a break room in a building with a flat roof. To the left, a narrow hall led to the offices. Judith went to the bulletin board next to the entrance and with a single glance registered that no one was still on assignment except for Matthias, Josef and Frank, along with a small cleaning crew. It looked like a quiet weekend. She would take a shower, drink about four litres of water and then make her way to her apartment, where she only had to collect her telescope and sleeping bag. She went over to her locker and removed her duffel bag, which contained the essentials for becoming a human again after a day like this.

After the shower she dried herself off and paused briefly in front of the mirror in the bathroom. She lowered the towel she had just used to rub down her hair. What did someone like Kai see in her? A woman who had, at some point, missed the exit marked 'pretty' and come to a rest with a stuttering motor next to 'mousey.' Only with great effort did she make progress on this bumpy road called life. She had already choked the motor completely a couple of times; the last time it looked like she had totalled it. She had to watch out. Every day, again and again. Not become complacent. Always keep in mind that the next exit could be marked 'terminus.' The fact that real work wasn't about an eight-hour shift, but how you coped with sixteen hours. She had already survived two years and was stuck in one lane at work. She forced herself not to avert her gaze as long as she could. Then she turned away and slipped into her jeans and an old but clean T-shirt. She returned to her locker with the bag in hand.

'Dearest Judith.'

She needed a moment to register what those two words meant. Dombrowski had crept up in his plimsolls. His plump face beamed with fake joy over seeing her again, the grey locks spinning their way over his high forehead like wet spider webs. He looked a freshly bathed Buddha, even if he wasn't just emerging from the showers, like her, but from an office with no air conditioning.

No, she thought. *Simply no*. He raised his arms as if he wanted to apologise.

'We have a cold starter.'

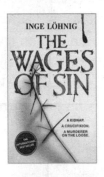